Trading Bright Lights For Lightning Bugs

Book 1 of the Small Town Girl Series

Jann Franklin

CONTENTS

CHAPTER 1—CITY GIRL INTERRUPTED

My father used to say, "Jen, life throws you curveballs. You just gotta keep swinging." I'd nod and smile, not realizing my father just delivered my biggest life lesson.

My childhood took place in a small town of twenty thousand people, and I hated every square mile. My friends and I spent Friday nights driving "the drag," the loop around downtown, laughing at the teens who trekked over from their even tinier towns. A town so small it didn't even have a drag? Thank goodness for small favors.

My number one college requirement was the city had a six-figure population. Baylor University fit my criteria. In a city of over two hundred thousand, I navigated one-way streets, a roundabout, and even multilevel highway access. My shopping expanded beyond JCPenney and Walmart to include an actual two-story mall. My culinary skills grew as well, and I embraced the joys of artisan bread and a salad bar in my grocery store.

After four years, I graduated and slid into an entry-level copywriting job in Dallas, Texas. Hello dear friend—where have you been all my life?

The sights and sounds beckoned me. "Jen, here we are! Just minutes from your doorstep." This girl had found her home! Yes, I could brush my teeth and cook breakfast at the same time in my tiny apartment. But I was fifteen minutes from my job. Hello, best life!

One fateful evening, I met my friends after work in a local bar. In typical rom-com movie fashion, my girlfriend brought along my future husband. As the new guy from her office, she'd forced Mike Guidry into a night out with his co-workers.

One look at those mocha eyes, the color of my favorite coffee drink, and there was no turning back. We talked for hours! Mike grew up in a tiny town outside of Baton Rouge, Louisiana. We both migrated to big cities, graduated college, and grabbed jobs in Dallas with dreams of making it big. We both had small-town values but big-city hearts. We were meant for each other.

A fairy tale wedding six months later in my hometown, with our mayor making an appearance. He'd gone to school with my grandfather, and there was a tale about a skunk in the principal's office. No one ever really knew the whole story, but it made my family small town royalty.

Mike and I honeymooned in the Caribbean, settling back to our routine as Mike and Jen Guidry. We saved and bought a house and planned our big city life together. Small towns were for visiting family, not for living. How can you survive without a decent cup of coffee less than ten minutes away?

Henry came into our lives a few years later, his life blessed with the choices and opportunities of a big city. My son wouldn't settle for the racks at the local retail stores. Henry would have the childhood I'd wished for myself.

My husband didn't share my enthusiasm. I'd exclaim opportunity, and Mike bemoaned the traffic. I rejoiced in my five choices of Chinese food, and he griped about the drive to get there. I chalked it up to fatigue and work stress, but I should have known better.

When James came along two years later, Mike's unhappiness filled our house. He'd earned a two-week hiatus between projects, so I expected a change. He wandered around, the field of creases in his forehead not budging. Was it work stress? Possibly a midlife crisis? Was Mike working out a plan to trade me in for a younger model? Maybe he'd come home with a Corvette or a motorcycle instead?

My brain shifted to Henry, about to start kindergarten in the fall. We had to choose a school and begin the application process. My list of prospects resided on my phone, warming my heart in our choices. Our menu ranged from progressive to charter to magnet to public to parochial. My kid had the world at his feet, and I had the list to prove it. But how to get my husband to sit down and narrow the playing field?

After dinner, we put the kids down for the night. Mike plopped on the couch, giving off a strange vibe. The dinner conversation concluded with everyone agreeing that Shaggy and Scooby definitely were the brains of the team, while Freddy and Daphne should be kicked out. My boys took cartoons quite seriously. Mike had no opinions about Velma's sleuthing skills, which struck me as odd. Normally, he had much to say about cartoon characters. Maybe he was eager to go over my kindergarten pros and cons list?

Just after we sat on the couch, but before I pulled out my list, my father's prophetic words came back to haunt me.

"Jen, I've really got to talk to you. There's something on my mind I need to say, but I don't think you're going to like it."

Where did that anvil come from and why was it planted on my heart? This was it—I was being traded in for a younger, flatter model. Was I ready to start swinging at the curveballs?

"Jen, I'm so unhappy. I hate my job, and I hate living in this house with its tiny yard. Every day I go to work and...I can't breathe! All I do is think back to when I was younger, and how much better my life was. This life we've got isn't working for me."

Steady Jen, get that huge weight off your heart. When Mike was younger? Did he mean when he was single? No, that heaviness on my heart was a foot. Mike's foot was planted on top of my chest. No wonder I couldn't breathe.

"Babe, there's this store in my hometown. It's called Big Ed's Parts 'n' More, and it's for sale. I want us to buy Big Ed's and move to my hometown, so I can run it."

Was that a gust of wind, or a sigh of relief from Mike? That second gust was definitely me. Yes! I was not being traded in for a newer model! There would be no Corvette or Harley in my driveway, either. We were going to be okay!

Whoosh! Reality hit, and a smaller weight returned to my chest. Within ten minutes of my home, I could purchase a movie ticket at seven movie theaters. Twenty restaurants awaited my order. The countdown to my big city days had started with Mike's announcement.

Lisa Douglas from the television show *Green Acres* said it best. *You are my wife. Goodbye, city life. Green Acres we are there.*

My mouth opened to protest, but Mike's face reflected pure joy. This was no city guy. My husband was a small-town man dressed in khakis and a golf shirt. Oh, how I adored this man with my very soul! He would die a little more each day if we stayed in Dallas. As much as I loved the bright lights, I had to give them up. For the love of my life, I would trade them in for lightning bugs. Goodbye city life. Graisseville we are there.

Graisseville (GRACE-VILLE), Louisiana, with a population of less than five hundred. The men in my life discussed trees and open spaces. Mike began telling childhood stories, playing outside until the lightning bugs came out. Running until he couldn't breathe. Our boys would create those same memories, running and playing until they were out of breath. As a mom of boys five and three, I recognized the benefits of sending my kids outside to just run. But how far would I have to go for a good cup of coffee?

CHAPTER 2-YOU WANT ME TO LIVE WHERE?

In typical small-town efficiency, Mike's cousin the realtor listed Big Ed's Parts 'n' More, and his buddy from high school handled our escrow. Those connections made us the proud owners of Big Ed's in record time. We scrambled to get our house on the market and took a long weekend to find our new home in Graisseville.

I'd lived in a big city all my adult life. Maybe going back to small-town living wouldn't be so bad. The boys would have room to run, we'd be near my in-laws and free babysitting, and our expenses could be less too. Be optimistic, Jen—excited even. Life throws you curveballs. Keep swinging girl!

After three weeks of house hunting, my options were bleak. Even worse than when my mom took me to the tractor supply to pick out a homecoming dress. Most homes for sale were in the historic district, with turn-of-the-century crown molding, mahogany paneled bedrooms, and dainty built-in shelves. The fancy trimmings would never stand against our rowdy boys.

We turned to outside Graisseville village limits, properties with sturdy floors and walls. Homes with little historical significance that could withstand Tonka trucks hitting the walls and Playdough flushed down the toilet. As small-town living loomed in front of me, my uneasiness grew. Where would I savor a cup of caffeinated heaven? Would I purchase all my clothes at Big Ed's, along with my plumbing and hardware? Would Henry and James have friends other than Joe-Bob or Bubba?

Mike called from Graisseville to talk houses. He had been running Big Ed's as soon as we closed on the property—farmers and ranchers don't take time off. Living on his parents' couch with his dad handing out helpful new business owner advice, Mike was beyond eager to find our new home.

"Jen, I've got three houses to look at just outside of town. Go to your computer—I'm sending you pictures right now."

Racing to my desk practically gave me a heart attack. As my breathing slowed, I turned to my friend Google. Typing the search phrase *Graisseville, Louisiana*, brought forth a million results. My heart leaped to break free of my ribcage, then sunk back into its spot as I studied my search. Most results beckoned me to visit Louisiana, not Graisseville. The bottom of the page stirred my soul—the Arts and Music Festival in nearby Zachary. Culture and entertainment only fifteen minutes from my new hometown! Google threw a kink in my plans to be the next power couple of Graisseville, however. My new hometown boasted 298 residents. Did a population that size even have power couples? Or coffee for that matter?

The room started spinning. Who took the oxygen? Did Graisseville have enough oxygen for four more people? You can't do this, Jen! Deep breaths...calm down. Maybe Mike could commute? Four hours wasn't that bad.

No, we needed to be together as a family. We had to make the situation work. Ping! Mike's email popped on my screen. This was getting real.

As I studied the photos labeled Property Number One, my trained eye picked up an important detail. "Uh, Mike. The first property doesn't have a house. Would we be living in tents? Maybe with some solar panels and a latrine? How exactly would that work?" What would Lisa Douglas do? She'd never leave New York City, that was certain.

"Yeah, it's just land. We'd stay with Mom and Dad or maybe rent a camper. But we'd get to build whatever kind of house we want. Just think Jen—you could design and build your dream home!"

"Yes, and in the meantime, I'd be living a nightmare—either sharing a bathroom with your parents or in fifteen feet of space with a man...and two men in training. Next!"

The pictures for Property Number Two featured a two-story Tudor-style home with a wide front porch. Just the place to drink my coffee and solve the world's problems! Four bedrooms, four bathrooms, two acres. "Mike, this house is perfect! Let's put in an offer before someone grabs it."

"Well, there might be a slight problem. It's less than a mile from the parish dump."

"Next!"

Property Number Three was literally a horse barn. "Mike! A barn, seriously? That's worse than living in a camper!"

"Jennifer Guidry! Aren't you forgetting Jesus was born in a stable? That's basically a barn, you know. Are you telling me you're better than Jesus?"

After seven years of marriage, my husband could feel a glare through the phone.

"Fine, Jen. We don't have to look at it."

And after seven years of marriage, I picked up on Mike's frustration over the phone lines. "No, you're right, honey. Let's look at the replica of our Lord and Savior's birth-place."

Were my standards too high? Unreasonable maybe? Three bedrooms, two bathrooms, an extra bedroom for guests, and a large backyard with a couple of acres. Ideally, a storage shed or third garage for assorted bikes, tools, lawn mower, etc. If I was giving up my big city life, then I wanted my dream home! My mother's voice drifted into my head.

"Jennifer, marriage is about compromise. That means you don't always get your way. Sometimes you will give up more than you think is fair. But you must set aside your desires and look at what is best for your family. Because, in the end, what is best for your family is best for you." Darn mothers!

What was best for my family? A mother who whined and complained until she got her dream home, driving the father to the brink of frustration in the process? Or a mother who thanked God for her blessings, that she would have a roof over her head and food on her table, no matter the size of said roof or table? Thank You, Lord, for mothers who give their children good advice.

As we toured the barn next to a one-room farmhouse we made our plans. The property came with five acres and a shed to store our belongings. The owner recently built the barn, so it was in great shape and could easily be changed. We'd live in the farmhouse while we renovated the barn. Our new home was only ten minutes from Big Ed's. It was the best option for our family, and the boys couldn't wait to tell their friends they would be living in a barn.

My curiosity got the better of me. "Why is this property for sale? With a brand new barn, I'd think the owners planned to say awhile."

Mike's cousin chuckled. "Well, when Arthur took out a loan to build on the property, his wife, Maryann, thought it was to make the house bigger. She was all fired up to start a family, and she took that as a sign that Arthur was too. But you see, Arthur took the loan and built a brand new, state of the art barn. Then he bought some fancy thoroughbred horses, making big plans to breed them. Oh boy, that was bad news for poor Arthur! Why Maryann, she told Arthur it was her or the horses. Now Arthur, well, he told Maryann that he'd need a good night's sleep to think about that. When Arthur woke up the next morning, Maryann had packed up and settled in at her mother's. So Arthur, well he jumped in his truck and high-tailed it over to my office. Told me he's gotta sell this place real quick, or Maryann might never come home."

"Well, if you get the chance to talk to Maryann, please give her a hug from me!"

Mike's cousin grinned. "Jen, this is a small town. You'll get the chance to do that yourself!"

Remember those girls in high school that always tried to fix up their friends? "You'll love going out with Debbie because she has a great personality." We all knew that was code for fat or ugly. And that's what I thought when I looked at the barn that was going to be our home. It had a great personality. It was probably very nice and stayed home most Saturday nights too.

Many evenings I repeated my mother's words. *Jen, marriage is about compromise.* We put an offer on the home with a great personality. It started to grow on me—like a homely dog that followed us home, so we decided to keep it.

Once we'd purchased our new residence, we worked quickly to sell our old one. Our neighbor, Phil, had always been a bit nosey, but he became downright stalking once the *For Sale* sign landed in our front yard.

"Now don't worry, Jen. I'll be sure and chat up anybody that comes by to look at your home. Think of me as your gatekeeper—I'll make sure just the right people become my new neighbors." No truer words were spoken.

We had had a lot of showings but no offers the first two weeks on the market, so I called my agent.

"Jen, I'm not sure how to tell you this, but one of your neighbors has inserted himself into the selling process. This person flies out his front door as soon as the potential buyers arrive. He introduces himself and delivers outrageous issues about your house. Crazy stuff, ranging from crime in the neighborhood to undisclosed flood and termite damage. I'm just not sure what to do."

My poor agent! "Thanks for letting me know, and don't give it another thought. In fact, I'm headed over there right now to take care of the problem."

No, Jen—make a cup of coffee first. After all, you need to figure out where to hide the body.

No doubt Phil was the troublesome neighbor, but what was the best strategy? Murder was still illegal in all fifty states, even if I did find a good place to hide the evidence.

Two cups of coffee later, I marched over to Phil's house. Three knocks later the door remained closed. The man never left his home, but he had one of those security systems with an app on his phone. My neighbor definitely knew who was on his doorstep.

"Phil! I know you're in there! Either open the door and talk to me face to face or talk to me on your app thingy!"

Arms crossed and angry glare planted firmly on my face, I waited.

Phil took the coward's way out. "Oh, hey, Jen! I'm sorry, I couldn't figure out how to answer you with my app."

You've got to be kidding me! That man spent the last block party showing off all the bells and whistles on that stupid security system. Mike developed a headache and left early, sticking me with Phil and his twenty-minute demonstration.

"Look, Phil, I know what you've been saying to our potential buyers. You'd better tell me what's going on, or I'll tell all the neighbors how you've been sabotaging our showings."

As I waited for an answer, I heard Phil's automatic sprinklers come on. The guy couldn't resist anything with an automatic timer.

"Okay, well here's the deal. Remember my son Theo? He and his wife Millie are looking to buy a home, and they'd like to be near me and my wife so we can babysit. Now, they really like your house, but they can't exactly afford your inflated price. So, I was just kinda hoping you might be more reasonable if you didn't have any offers."

Yeah, Phil, that was a wise move to talk over the security system. If he'd answered the door, Mike might have been bailing me out of jail.

"Look here, Phil. We've got a new house in Louisiana, and we've got to get this one sold. For the price we've listed, okay? You better stop your shenanigans immediately, or I will let everyone in the neighborhood know what you're doing. And you will never receive an invitation to another neighborhood gathering. Not even the community cleanup! Do you understand me, Phil?"

Phil lived for those parties—it was the only time people would talk to him. No, Phil would not be sabotaging our home sale.

Our amazing agent emailed her peers, explained the case of the nosey neighbor, and hosted a fabulous open house for all of them. She sprung for wine, some high-class appetizers, a three-tiered dessert tray, and the most delectable lemon Bundt cake. Within two weeks, we had five offers. Thirty days later, we said goodbye to the bright lights of Dallas.

CHAPTER 3 – MOVING AND PREGNANCY ARE TOO SIMILAR

O ur church offered to help us move, and we jumped at the offer. Early one Saturday morning, eleven people arrived to load the rented moving truck. We had a washer and dryer, my great-grandmother's buffet, a refrigerator, and an antique rolltop desk. Not to mention the assorted beds, toys, bikes, etc.

My friend Tracy found one of my unmentionables on the kitchen counter—it had been behind the washer and dryer, retrieved by the men when they moved the appliances. After spending some time guessing which men saw my undergarment, Tracy resolved my fears.

"Jen, those panties are in great shape, an attractive size, and look really nice. Girl, you should be proud." Oh, I was going to miss Tracy terribly.

Someone assured me unpacking was much better than packing, but she was delusional. Moving is like being pregnant. People come out of the woodwork with stories and advice that really aren't helpful, and the pain really is as bad as you think it's going to be (sometimes worse). You should definitely spread them out, so you can forget the bad parts and focus on the excitement. It also takes longer than you think to get down the new routine. Moving is more expensive than you expect too, just like having a baby. Our refrigerator was a perfect example. We moved it from Dallas, plugged it in, and discovered it didn't work anymore. Maybe it couldn't bear to leave Dallas, either. *Buy a new refrigerator* moved to the top of my ever-growing to-do list. Those were the joys of moving.

Mike couldn't close up Big Ed's to go refrigerator shopping, so I left the boys with Mike's mom, Ava, and headed out to Baton Rouge, population 227,470. Baton Rouge was the closest place to purchase a refrigerator, and it was definitely my kind of town.

Buying a new refrigerator didn't grace my top ten list of favorite activities, but I mentally dangled coffee as my reward. A good cup of coffee will motivate me to do most anything. My plan was to settle for the first decent refrigerator, then reward myself with a caffeinated beverage. Was that coffee calling my name?

As I pulled into a well-known national chain store, I marveled at the hundred-foot banner. The store boasted the largest selection of appliances this side of Lake Pontchartrain! My new bestie Marty led me to a fantastic deal on a refrigerator, and I patted myself on the back for my mad shopping skills. My pride retreated when Marty rang up my ticket.

"Now, Mrs. Guidry, I just need your address, so I can schedule your delivery."

Of course, Marty could have my home address! After all, we had just bonded in the large appliance section, and I counted Marty among my new friends in Louisiana.

"Why, yes, Marty, it's 227 Abington Road, Graisseville. The zip is 70820."

My new friend stopped typing and looked at me strangely. "You don't live in Baton Rouge?"

Why did I have the feeling I wasn't getting my new refrigerator any time soon?

"No, Marty, I don't. Is that a problem?"

Marty's smile headed for the nearest door marked Exit, right on the heels of his commission.

"Well, Mrs. Guidry, we only deliver within the Baton Rouge city limits. However, you can take your refrigerator home with you today. Do you have a truck or trailer so you can haul it home?"

My heart sank as I thought of my Jeep Wrangler in the parking lot. No way was I calling Mike. His Saturday-at-the-store tales always ended with "and I never even got to go to the bathroom." No, best to call my father-in-law.

"Jen, sweet girl! How's your trip to the big city?" I just loved my father-in-law, mostly because he adored me and would do anything for me.

"Hey Walt, I've run into a bit of a problem. I need your help."

As I outlined my dilemma, Walt listened carefully.

"Jenny, Mike should have told you. Nobody delivers appliances to Graisseville. You always have to take them home yourself."

Thanks, Walt. I could have used that piece of valuable information about four hours ago.

"Nah, see you have to bring your own truck or trailer to haul it home. I would offer my truck, but it's in the shop. And we just have Ava's minivan. Maybe you could trade vehicles with Mike? Bring his truck to the city to pick up your refrigerator. I'd help you, but my back isn't what it used to be. And I don't think I could do it."

My heart sank as I struggled to find a ride home for my beloved appliance.

Walt wasn't finished helping, though. "You could hire Roby Melancon to pick up your fridge! He's done it before for other people. Now ol' Roby will try to charge you $400 to drive to the big city. Because of the traffic and all. But don't you let him! You use that fancy college degree in communications, and you get him down to $200. Let me give you his number."

My father-in-law would give you the shirt off his back, but he'd have to make some sideways comment about you as payment. In my case, it was my college degree in communications. One Christmas I overheard Walt talking to his brother. "Well, I just don't understand why someone would have to go to college for four whole years, just to learn to communicate! If everybody's speaking the same language, it's pretty darn easy. Why I do it every day!"

As I ended my call to Walt, I channeled my fancy college degree talents. "Hello, Roby! This is Jennifer Guidry, Walt Guidry's daughter-in-law. I've got a job for you, and I'm hoping you can do it for $200."

Unfortunately, Roby had the upper hand since he had the truck. "Well, ma'am, Baton Rouge is a long way. And with gas prices the way they are, I'd have to charge $350 to pick up something that large and haul it all the way to Graisseville. And pull it off my truck and bring it into your house. But since you're kin to Walt, I could do it for $200."

Sic 'em Bears and my degree in communications!

"But it will be two weeks from Monday. That work for you?"

Two weeks without a refrigerator? Roby might as well have asked if I could go two weeks without breathing.

"How much to deliver my refrigerator on Monday?"

"Well, ma'am, I already promised Moe Gladstone I'd clean out his gutters and mow his lawn. And Lila Trahan, well she's promised me $200 if I clean out her garage. Plus another $200 bonus if I do it Monday. So I really couldn't do it for less than $400. On account of that bonus and all."

My refrigerator wasn't such a great deal, and I regretted my prideful text to Mike. My quest for a good cup of coffee reached critical stages.

Marty brightened considerably when his commission walked back in the front door. "You have a good day, Mrs. Guidry—come back again soon!" Not if I could help it, Marty.

Turning to my most important mission, I pulled up my navigation app. I was a coffee snob and I had no shame about it. Local coffee shops revved my engine, and I didn't shy away from an expensive cup of happiness. This girl was worth a cup of high-dollar coffee, and that day was no exception.

Google Maps pointed me to Cuppa Joe's on Perkins Road. Five-star reviews and unique coffee blends reassured my coffee-deprived nerves. Mardi Gras and Strawberries 'n' Cream? Yes, please! And when was the last time I'd had such a physical need for coffee? Please, Lord, don't let my impatience cause an accident. Please give me a quick but safe ride to my caffeine haven.

The moment my tennis shoes hit the doorway, my nostrils experienced the sweet smells of coffee and pastries. Ah, my tribe, my wonderful coffee tribe! Life was good again.

"A large King Cake coffee and, what the heck? I'll take a beignet too." Say what you will about Louisiana, but those people know how to cook!

My second friend in Louisiana made my drink and chatted me up. Josie studied interior design at LSU and promised to send me some ideas for my new home. She urged me to purchase bags of King Cake coffee too. "You'll thank me later, Jen, as you're sipping a cup this evening."

We parted ways all too soon, but my new friend texted me a list of local home furnishing stores, so I could turn our temporary digs into something a little homier.

Fortified with caffeine, I dropped $300 on wall art to spruce up our one room. We'd left most everything in storage, so I wanted to give our temporary home some style.

My hour's drive back to Graisseville flew by as I mentally reviewed my purchases and envisioned them in my one-room home. According to my calculations, I'd created a backdrop of Southern living on a budget. Perhaps I'd invite New Orleans-born actress, Reese Witherspoon to my soon-to-be-fashionably decorated home!

The sign for the Dairy Delight popped into my eye line, and I heard the siren call of tater tots and tea. A call to Ava confirmed I'd be a little later than originally planned, but I'd scored some amazing purchases. As I hung up the phone, I felt eyes boring into my back. Were those people by the door whispering about me? A quick glance at my clothes and shoes confirmed nothing was out of place. Best to go to the bathroom for a closer look, just in case.

A click confirmed I'd locked the stall, and I gave myself a thorough inspection. No toilet paper stuck to my shoe, no underwear peeking out of my waistband, nothing inappropriate showing. What the heck? As I exited the stall I glanced in the mirror over the sink. Ponytail in place. Wait, were ponytails unacceptable in Graisseville? Jen, you're imagining things—go get your tater tots!

A high school student took my order and handed me my receipt. She walked over to the fry cook and whispered in his ear as he stared at me. They had to be talking about me! As I drank my diet root beer, I felt eyes boring into my soul. After five minutes, I got my tots and fled the Dairy Delight. Ugh, I should have gone through the drive-thru.

As I pulled into Walt and Ava's driveway, I shoved the Dairy Delight experience into the back of my head. Focus on your new stuff Jen! Won't Ava be impressed at my clever shopping bargains?

My mother-in-law, Ava was a true Southern lady, and her love language had always been food. My main concern when I joined the family was my waistline, so I'd spent most family gatherings in bed or in the bathroom. Not surprisingly, Mike's family found me thin and sickly. As the years passed, I confessed my true feelings to Ava. But she never stopped devising ways to force-feed her sugar creations.

Ava's motto, *one bite won't hurt*, worked only if she offered one bite. The woman was a baking machine, and she created a steady stream of goods every week. There were always parties, church functions, barbecues, weddings, funerals, bridal, and baby showers. She also baked for neighbors feeling poorly or down on their luck. Ava truly believed that a sweet creation could literally cure anything that ails, physical or emotional. My mother-in-law made it her life's mission to make me sample every baked good coming out of her oven.

Henry and James jumped at the chance to go to Granny's house. We had lived here just a week or so, and those kids had figured out Granny was not aware of the word no. How would I survive Ava and her shower of baked goods? My brain was still planning a strategy. This time, however, I would stay for a cup of coffee and "just one bite." Showing Ava my purchases and sharing my day with her was more important. Besides, I'd already had a beignet and tater tots. The diet had been blown.

Ava greeted me at the door with a ball-shaped cookie dusted with powdered sugar.

"Hello, sweet girl! Try a pecan and butterscotch ball cookie. Margie Taylor's cousin's grandmother passed, so I'm going to take these over to the family."

Small-town births, illnesses, and deaths were marked by food. Ava didn't miss a single opportunity to celebrate or grieve. I loved her for that, I truly did. As I chose a chair at the kitchen table, I pulled my full cup of coffee towards me. Ava had set the sugar bowl and cream pitcher close by. The woman got me—she really did. I tolerated milk in my coffee but preferred cream. Ava had placed pecan butterscotch balls in the middle of the table. As I nibbled on the one received at the door, I poured the cream in my coffee. Jen, you can do it! Just say no. Who was I kidding? That was a losing battle. Just offer to take some home for Mike and the boys.

"Jenny, tell me all about your trip to the big city! Mike didn't tell you to bring a way to haul your new refrigerator home? I know Mike's busy with Big Ed's store, but he needs to take care of his family."

What? According to Ava, Mike walked on water, for the most part. Had critical words of her firstborn ever exited the woman's lips? Not to my knowledge. Well, except for the girls he'd dated before me.

"Oh, thank goodness Mike married a respectable young lady. Not like that Sarah girl back in high school. Between you and me Jenny, Sarah didn't have the best reputation in the neighborhood. And oh, those two grandbabies! They are the light of my life. If only Joe would get married and have some kids."

Thanks to Mike's previous girlfriend, his brother Joe, and my boys, my status as the best daughter-in-law ever was solid.

"No worries, Ava. Roby and I struck a deal. But let's talk about the rest of my trip!" Best to steer the subject away from my lack of negotiation skills and move right on to my purchases. As I gave Ava a full accounting of my trip to the big city and showed off my treasures Vanna White style, Ava's eyes darkened. To my dismay, she wasn't thrilled about my new home décor.

"Okay, spill it, Ava. What's the matter?"

My mother-in-law hesitated. "Jenny girl, you know I love you. I think you are so good for Mike, and you gave me those beautiful grandbabies. Lord knows Mike's brother Joe can't be bothered to settle down and produce any offspring. Walt and I are very grateful you've given up your big city life to live here near us. We are just delighted we get to see those grandbabies any time we want."

Okay, Ava, I know there's a *but* coming soon. "We really want you to fit in and feel happy and make friends and all. We want you to love Graisseville as much as we do. But..."

Yep, that was overdue. "When you go to the big city to buy things, people may think you're being uppity. You know, thinking you're too good for the things we have for sale here."

Huh? "But, Ava, Mike said I had to go to Baton Rouge to buy our refrigerator." What in the world?

"Yes, sweetie, that is true. But we have local artists and opportunities here that offer home decor and furnishings. I am just suggesting that in the future, you look here first for what you want before traveling so far to the big city."

A smile crept onto my face, like a cat trying to sneak onto a lap. Everyone referred to Baton Rouge as *the big city,* and I just vacated a city over five times that size.

"Okay, I'm confused. This town doesn't even have three hundred people, with no mall or even a shopping center. Where are these local artists?"

Her smile never wavered, as if she was talking to a small child. Or a foreigner who knows nothing about local culture. Which category did I fall into?

"Jenny, we have many artists and craftsmen who sell their merchandise out of local businesses. The Gas 'n' More has some wall art and even clothes for sale. In fact, Mike has clothing and home furnishings in Big Ed's. You just tell me what you're looking for, and I can point you in the right direction."

Buying clothes at the same place Mike got fertilizer? Patience, Jen. "Tell me what I need to do, so no one thinks I'm being uppity."

Keep the edge out of your voice, girl! Take a gulp of coffee. Maybe another pecan ball thingies? No, stay strong—you might need one later in the conversation.

"I'm so glad you asked! We have an up-and-coming artist who's been featured in the Graisseville *Gazette.* She works in oils, and she's just brilliant! If you purchased one of her paintings for your home, your standing in the community would improve!"

But I was a Guidry and part owner of Big Ed's Parts 'n' More—wasn't that enough? Wow, I had a lot to learn about my new hometown.

"Okay, Ava, I'm game. Point me in the right direction. Where do I go to buy one of these paintings?" Lord, help me get this over as soon as possible.

"You're in luck! Mike sells some paintings on consignment down at Big Ed's. You can go down there and pick one out!"

"Sounds great! I'll stop in next week and pick one up."

Two pecan ball creations later, my kids and I headed home.

As we sat down for dinner that night, I relayed my conversation with Mike's mother. He wasn't surprised. "No big revelation there, Jen. The artist, Eula Mae Bergeron Fontenot, is a direct descendant of one founding father. And she married a direct descendent of another. Those founding families carry a lot of weight around here."

Ah, this was all starting to make more sense. A painting from Eula Mae would definitely help me fit in better. And make up for the fact I wasn't born and raised in Louisiana.

"Great! So grab one of the paintings and bring it home on Monday. Problem solved!"

Just a slight hesitation. "Uh, you know, babe, I really don't feel comfortable choosing our home décor—that's always been your department. Why don't you come down to the store and chose one yourself?"

Mike rarely fit in time for bathroom breaks, much less choosing a fine work of art. Was this his way of politely saying no?

"Not a problem. You know, I haven't been down to the store, anyway. According to Louisiana community property law, that place is half mine. Maybe it's time for me to inspect my property."

"Sure, honey. Could you pass the potatoes?" The end of another enlightening marital conversation. It beat trying to guess how many pecan balls Henry ate at Granny Ava's.

Between Mike's exhaustion and my reluctance to socialize without a Eula Mae work of art, we skipped church on Sunday. On Monday, the kids and I dropped by Big Ed's. My promise of peanut butter and honey sandwiches like Granny's practically guaranteed a smooth visit. Moms use incentives, not bribery, to encourage their children to behave. At least, that's what we tell ourselves so we can sleep at night.

We breezed through the front doors and headed toward the back of the store, where Mike was patiently explaining the difference between pre-diluted and concentrated antifreeze. Who said my husband led a boring life?

I caught something out of the corner of my eye, something jarring like a traffic accident. A traffic accident so horrific I couldn't look away but was mesmerized by the sight.

Just to the right of the back doors taking up approximately fifty square feet were the most grotesque, misshapen, startlingly surreal oil paintings I had ever seen. Mike and I had been members of the Museum of Modern Art, so we'd viewed all sorts of ugly and bizarre art. Those collections would never be in the same league as the monstrosities before me. Ah hah! This was the real reason Mike wouldn't choose a painting for our home. He was as repulsed as I was.

"Boys, let's head to the toy tractor section." Think, Jen think—you need a plan! Ugh, I had nothing. Would peeking over the aisle, thirty feet away, maybe with just one eye, soften the view? Nope, those assaults to the art world were just as horrendous thirty feet away as they had been at three feet.

Mike spotted me across the store and jogged over. "I guess you've seen Eula Mae's paintings," His grin plastered his face like a billboard.

As the boys played with the toy trucks and hay balers, we put our heads together.

"How much are these paintings?"

"Honey, the better question is...how uppity does the town think you are? And are you willing to live with that?"

Reading between the lines told me I had a decision to make. How much would I spend to be accepted fully into the Graisseville fold?

"Well, according to your mom, the town thinks I'm extremely uppity. So yeah, we'd better get the biggest, ugliest painting. How much is your consignment fee? We can subtract that from the price."

Mike blew a gust of air that would knock down a house of cards. "Actually, Jen, I'm doing it as a favor to Eula Mae's son, Justin. We went to high school together and..."

Yeah, I knew the drill. He was a buddy, and Mike was helping him out by putting his mom's horrendous paintings in the store. I could respect that, helping a friend. But that didn't help our finances. The move took a toll on our savings account, and we wanted the proceeds from the sale to go straight to our barn renovations.

"Could we commission Eula Mae to paint a picture of your Grandmother Guidry? We could score more points for a commission, and maybe the painting would be less hideous. Since it would be of a family member?"

Mike wrapped me in his arms like a warm overcoat. "Jen, that's a great idea! Maybe I can get Justin to talk his mom into discounting the price. You know, since I'm letting her use valuable floor space to peddle her paintings."

Should we high-five or smack each other's butts? Or whatever it is people do when they've concocted a fabulous plan and saved the day. In the end, we kissed goodbye, and the boys and I went home to our peanut butter and honey sandwiches.

Mike and Justin hammered out a deal. Ava provided a lovely photograph of Grand-mother Guidry. The local grapevine made it known Mike and Jen Guidry had commis-sioned a painting from Eula Mae. It was a win for all involved. That was until I had to hang it in my home. Ah, the sacrifices we make for the ones we love.

CHAPTER 4 – BIG ED'S NEWEST EMPLOYEE

T he more hours Mike worked at the store, the more I understood why Big Ed retired. His sons had helped him out, but they retired with their dad. Our boys couldn't reach the cash register, so they wouldn't be helping anytime soon. Mike hadn't taken any time off since we purchased the store. For my husband's health and my sanity, he had to find some help.

The store was closed on Sundays, but there was always someone with an emergency.

"Hey, Mike! Can you meet me at the store? I gotta get this hay in, and my baler needs spark plugs." Farmers and ranchers didn't take time off, and neither did their parts 'n' more supplier. The day Mike left early to be home for supper or opened late to have breakfast with the family would be the day his customers went somewhere else.

I had taken my job because it was flexible, and let me work from home. Although it was ideal while the kids were young, flexibility didn't pay the bills. We had always used my income for the extra stuff like vacations and eating out. At that moment in our lives, only the kids and I enjoyed the extra stuff. Mike worked sixty hours a week to pay our bills.

Twenty minutes after pulling into the driveway, Mike hugged the boys, then cruised off to Snoresville by way of the couch. As the concerned and loving wife, I promoted myself to the store hiring committee.

"What about putting an ad in the paper, honey?"

Mike shook his head. "You just don't get it. I'm not going to find a reliable employee with a random ad that just anyone can answer. I've got to ask around, talk to the locals, find out who they recommend."

Nope, I didn't get it. Why was there a local paper with a classifieds section if we couldn't use it?

"Besides, Jen, I've got someone starting tomorrow. Tip Holloway's kid, Trip. He's graduated high school and is enrolled in *E* Burp. He wants to run his own business someday. He'll be great."

Many kids graduating from the local high schools enrolled in East Baton Rouge Parish Community College—or EBRPCC. That abbreviation only had one vowel, so people called it *E* Burp. My children would never darken the doors of *E* Burp. Our family newsletter would never proclaim the kids attended a place named after a bodily function.

Mike wasn't the only Guidry needing help. My projects had been hitting my boss' inbox at 2:00 a.m. Despite best efforts, I couldn't find a local daycare or babysitter. My mother-in-law enjoyed watching the boys but made it clear she had a life beyond her grandbabies.

"Don't forget, Jenny—I have bridge club and ladies' prayer circle. Not to mention all the baking and cooking I do for the community. My babysitting time is limited, especially during the day."

With my husband chained to Big Ed's, I was functioning on little sleep. My motivation hit an all-time high—Mike had to find a reliable employee to take up some slack, and I had to find a full-time babysitter. My motivation pushed me out the door to arrive at Big Ed's on Trip's first day. Boys and travel mug full of coffee, I was a force to be reckoned with. My force was very much needed.

Trip Holloway was very cute, very polite, and very much knew nothing about any type of parts—tractor or otherwise. He sent Moe Gladstone to the wrong side of the store looking for hydraulic fluid. Ben Wheeler needed propane, but Trip sent him to the front of the store to sort through dog food. My poor husband! Mike was trying to keep up, doing his best to soothe customers' irritations. It was a train wreck, for sure.

Then Amy Melancon and her son, Jimmy, walked into my life. "Hey, Mike! Me and Jimmy are looking for a ratchet set for Ken." She relaxed her hand on Jimmy's arm.

Jimmy faced the back, surveying his kingdom. "Mama, aisle two, middle, on the bottom shelf." Jimmy was so confident in his tone that I couldn't help but believe him.

His military cut and discount clothes added to his authenticity, and he looked just like all the other customers milling around the store. Mike backed me up on my beliefs.

"Hey, Jimmy! Yep, you're right, aisle two." No doubt Mike smiled for the first time that morning.

As Jimmy waited for his mom to check out, he gave directions to every person walking through the doors. My initial vibe was correct—Jimmy knew the entire layout of the store. Poor Trip knew all the cheerleaders by name but could not give a recommendation for the best galvanized stock tank. He was no match for Jimmy. At the end of Amy's shopping experience, Jimmy had pointed more customers toward their farming and ranching needs than poor Trip could ever hope to achieve. Jimmy was destined to be the next Big Ed's employee—but how to help Mike see it that way? If Amy got on board, the idea could work. My coffee and me, we had this.

My feet did double time to catch Amy as she walked out the door. We'd never met, but the woman was the answer to my prayers.

"Hello! I'd like to introduce myself, I'm Mike Guidry's wife, Jen."

Amy stared at me, eyes squinting at my ignorance. "Oh, I know who you are! Everyone in town knows who you are, honey. I'm Amy Melancon, and this is my boy, Jimmy." Her narrow smile reflected amusement. Silly girl, thinking this woman didn't know me!

Jump right in, Jen, before she tells you what people are saying about me.

"It's so nice to meet you, Amy! You too, Jimmy! I'm so impressed with your knowledge of the store, Jimmy. Have you ever considered working here at Big Ed's?"

Amy chuckled. Was she contemplating my sanity? "Jimmy baby, why don't you wait in the car? Me an' Mrs. Guidry are going to have a little talk."

The car door slammed, signaling Amy she could speak freely. "Mrs. Guidry, I'm going to assume you meant that kindly because I'm a Christian woman. And I like to think the best of everyone. So let me explain something to you. Jimmy is a good boy, but he's not the fastest mule in the barn, so to speak. He wouldn't be a good fit for the store."

Huh? My brain shifted into overtime. Okay, Jimmy was slow, but lots of people like him held jobs.

"Well, he knows the inventory as well as Mike—maybe even better. He can definitely help people find things in the store. Tell me what else Jimmy could do, if he worked in the store."

Just like the sun coming out after a thunderstorm, Amy's face brightened. Why of course! Amy had spent a great deal of time dealing with what Jimmy couldn't do. That proud mama was excited to tell someone what her son could do.

"Ok, Jimmy knows all the US currency. He knows dollar bills and fives and twenties. And even fifties and hundreds. He knows quarters and dimes and nickels and pennies. He can't figure out change, but the register does that. He can count out the change, I'm pretty sure. I don't know if he could run credit cards, but he can definitely ring up cash purchases." Amy's eyes sparkled like brightly polished pennies. Her voice rose half an octave and she spoke more quickly, excited about Jimmy's accomplishments.

"He helps his daddy on the farm, so he knows all about machine engines and how to fix them. Most of the people that come in here just want someone to help them find the parts and supplies. Jimmy can definitely help them with that."

Happiness bubbled out of Amy's voice, like a pot of gumbo simmering on the stove. The woman could see Jimmy's potential as Big Ed's next employee.

"Jimmy knows about feed and care for livestock. Most people coming into the store know what they need, so they just want someone to help them find it and ring it up. You know, Mrs. Guidry, I think maybe Jimmy could do it. I'm just not sure about the credit cards."

My shoulders slumped as I let out a breath deep enough to spin a pinwheel. "Please call me Jen and let me talk to Mike. Could you and Jimmy come back this evening, after the store closes?"

Another grin wider than the Sabine River. "Yes, ma'am, we sure can!"

Oh, please don't let my absence from the boys spell disaster. Henry and James were good for the most part, but they were boys. And boys without parental supervision could definitely be a problem.

Whew! No obvious damage. Mike was still chasing Trip, correcting his incorrect directions with various customers.

This would be easier than I'd hoped! A glance down Aisle One, toys and candy, made me pick up my pace. Maybe I should speed past? Could those kids belong to someone else? Nope, those shirts, despite the chocolate stains, looked too familiar. My boys had managed to eat their weight in chocolate candy bars. Aisle One looked suspiciously clean—where was the evidence? My tiny shoplifters had wiped their hands all over their clothes and stuffed the empty wrappers down their pants. As I scooped up James and grabbed Henry's hand, my brain calculated the distance to the parking lot. Could I clear the door before Mike noticed? A quick glance assured me I had nothing to worry about. My husband was giving ten percent discounts to customers returning from wild goose chases, courtesy of Trip.

Jeep parked, boys bathed, G-rated movie playing, then time to plan my strategy. Step One would definitely be getting Mike to admit Trip had no future at Big Ed's. Step One was fairly easy. Step Two would be getting Mike to realize what he needed an employee to do. If Mike could decide all he needed was someone to help people find items in the store and ring up their purchases, then he would willingly come with me to Step Three. That step, of course, was deciding whether Jimmy fit all the requirements of Step Two.

A call to Ava came next. "Could you watch the boys for a couple of hours, and feed them dinner?"

"Of course, Jenny! I'll send Walt over to get them, and they can pick up pizza at the Gas 'n' More." Did every successful business in town add *'n' More* as part of their expansion plan?

Butterflies had taken up residence in my stomach. Would this crazy plan work? It had to, for Mike's sake. And Jimmy's too.

Ava approved of my scheme and gave me some backstory on Jimmy. Shortly after Jimmy started school, his teacher and the school counselor confirmed what his parents feared: Jimmy had a below-average intelligence level. As Jimmy progressed through school, every expert repeated the diagnosis. Jimmy would never advance beyond sixth-grade knowledge and skills. His parents were devastated, but they never stopped helping him learn. They worked with their son and discovered he had an incredible memory. His father, Ken, taught him about farming, from farm machinery to farm animals. Jimmy remembered all of it. Ken had been taking Jimmy to Big Ed's since he was a boy, and Jimmy could find anything in the store.

Lord, I know You have a plan for this wonderful young man. If it could be Your will, could Your plan include working at Big Ed's?

Thank goodness for the Dairy Delight and their root beer floats. They were Mike's favorite and were essential to my plan. As I walked into Big Ed's and handed Mike his float, my heart hurt. In Dallas, I'd seen my husband look the most discouraged and exhausted he'd ever been. But that night he looked even worse.

My sweet husband flashed a tired smile and dug into his float. "Babe, how do you do it? You know exactly what I need, and you give it to me." He closed his eyes and sighed as he dipped another spoonful.

Should I feel guilty? My bribe had been misunderstood as an act of love. Maybe it was both. As I leaned against the counter beside him, Step One began.

"Honey, how was your day? How did Trip work out?"

Mike's shoulders stiffened like petrified wood. "I had to fire him. Geez, Jen, I felt horrible! But I seriously think he was relieved. Did you know he doesn't even want to own a business? His dad fed me that line to get me to hire him! He's majoring in music at *E* Burp. Music!"

Mike dipped his spoon again. Ugh! Why didn't I get a large? "What am I going to do? I can't run this store alone, and I don't know who else to hire."

A knock on the door and Mike's shoulders dragged the floor. "Not another customer!"

"I have an idea, sweetie." I tossed the words over my shoulder as I opened the glass door and ushered in Step Three. Dang it! I hadn't allowed enough time for Steps One and Two. I was going to have to put them all together.

"Mike, do you remember today how Jimmy knew where everything was in the store? He told everyone the right aisle and even where on the shelf. Do you remember that?"

Mike was no dummy. He knew where I was headed. "Yes, Jen, I do." He nodded at the Melancons and turned back to me. "But there's a lot more to working here than knowing the store layout. No offense, Amy."

Amy smiled, but it wasn't quite as bright as that morning. Dang it, Mike! He wasn't going to shoot down my brilliant plan before I unveiled all three steps.

"I'm going to ask you to do one thing, honey before you shoot down my idea. Show Jimmy how to use the cash register for a cash purchase. Then pretend to be a customer and test him."

Okay, two things. Amy's brilliant smile returned, with a confidence I'd not seen. Mike hesitated, then shrugged. "I'm not going to win this argument, am I? Jimmy, come over here."

A quick lesson, another spoonful of root beer float, and my husband strolled to the front door.

"Okay, Jimmy, I just walked in the door. What do you do?" Mike's voice sang with a cheerfulness his eyes refused to share.

"Welcome to Big Ed's Parts 'n' More, sir. How may I help you?"

Whoa! Both Mike and I caught ourselves staring open-mouthed at the young man.

Oh, Amy, you clever girl! You went home and came up with a strategy of your own. Honey, you might be my favorite new friend.

Mike gulped his ice cream and slid into the role of customer extraordinaire. "Son, I need five gallons of hydraulic fluid, and don't give me none of that premium crap. I ain't paying more money than I need to!"

Jimmy didn't blink. "No, sir, my daddy says the same thing. He don't believe in paying for a fancy name either. Aisle seven has hydraulic fluid. I'll show you what he always buys."

I caught Amy's eye as she beamed at me, the face of a proud mama. Mike and Jimmy disappeared down aisle seven, discussing the merits of hydraulic fluid. Two peas in a pod.

Two minutes later the men reappeared with a five-gallon bucket of all-season hydraulic fluid. Jimmy ambled to the cash register and mimicked Mike's instructions exactly. Mr. Customer Extraordinaire handed him two twenty-dollar bills and a five. Jimmy input the amount, put the money into the till, and glanced up at the register. He pulled out the change, counted it out to Mike, and thanked him for being a Big Ed customer. As Mike's forehead wrinkled, my heart pounded.

Amy couldn't help herself. "Now, Mike, I don't know that Jimmy can do credit cards. But he can ring up cash purchases with the best of them."

Mike put up a hand. "No, Amy, that's fine. I've been thinking about getting rid of credit cards and just doing farm accounts. You know, where customers put their expenses on account and I send a bill every month. Those dang credit card fees are killing me."

A half turn toward the man of the hour. "Son, if a customer doesn't pay cash, could you write his name and his purchase on a piece of paper for me?"

Jimmy met Mike's stare. "Yes, sir, I can read and write."

Amy interrupted. "Yeah, Mike, I'll work with him, and I'm sure he can do it. Also, I was thinking, if you do decide to hire him, I'll be willing to stay with him and make sure he does okay." She looked at Mike sideways, half afraid of the answer.

"Nah, that's okay, Amy. I'll be here, so if Jimmy has any problems, he can just ask me. We'll take it slowly as we go, but hopefully this young man will handle the store while I go to lunch with my incredibly intelligent and beautiful wife." Mike's grin was literally from ear to ear. "Amy, why don't you and I step into my office to talk hours and pay?"

They headed toward the back, and I was left with Jimmy.

My heart felt like melted ice cream, and I smiled at my hero. "Well, this is exciting, Jimmy! Your first paying job! I bet your dad is going to be so proud of you!"

"Yes, ma'am. I was wondering one thing, though."

Such a serious face! Keep your eyes straight ahead, Jen, and match his look. This young man had something important to say. Was Jimmy concerned about days off? A 401(k)? Maybe an employee discount?

Jimmy stared me straight in the eyes. "Do you think Mr. Mike would pay me in gum? See, I love gum, but Mama says I can only have two pieces a day because it's bad for my teeth. So I was thinking if Mr. Mike paid me in gum, then I could have as much as I wanted. And Mama couldn't say no since I earned it and all."

What a relief! "Jimmy, I'm sure we can work something out. You leave that to me." The kid just saved my husband's sanity. The least I could do was to be his gum dealer.

CHAPTER 5—TIME TO MEET THE TOWN

Meeting the town? No thank you! Ever since my mother-in-law told me shopping out of town made me look uppity, I knew I would never fit in. But dodging church and Ava's bridge club invitations had become exhausting. Hopefully, my stunning picture of Evelyn Guidry worked its magic. Not to mention my part in getting a job for Jimmy Melancon. In June, just four weeks after our big move, I was ready to start meeting the town by way of Graisseville Baptist Church.

Graisseville had two fine churches called Graisseville Baptist and Graisseville Methodist. Village history reported that originally both churches shared a pastor, which meant both Methodists and Baptists had worshiped together every Sunday. During that time, everyone worshiped at the Methodist Church on the first, third, and fifth Sundays, then at the Baptist Church on the second and fourth Sundays. Within the last twenty years, each church retained its own pastor as well as a bit of a rivalry.

Officially, it was all in good Christian fun, but certain rumors floating around told a different tale. One story involved an unnamed denomination stealing another denomination's peace lilies the Saturday night before Easter Sunday. The storyteller wouldn't give more details, but Ava often mentioned the year the Baptist church sanctuary was decked out in peace lilies. "Why, I imagine someone cleaned the flower stores out of all their lilies. It was just so beautiful!"

There was payback as well, according to my source. "Oh, revenge was sweet, let me tell you! All I will say is the community pancake breakfast hosted by the thieving denomination fell flat. What is breakfast without condiments or coffee?"

The Guidry family had always attended a Baptist Church, and that would never change, at least not in my lifetime. I grew up in a Presbyterian Church, and my future mother-in-law almost fainted when Mike and I took communion with real wine. I never told Ava that my maid of honor stocked the communion cups with Merlot from my parents' bar. Some things were best left unsaid.

So, there I stood, in the middle of my one-room home, Evelyn Guidry staring down at me in a field of flowers. James' hair stuck straight up like a cornfield, refusing my efforts to flatten the crop. Henry needed twenty-seven reminders to find his shoes and have Daddy help him tie the laces. Daddy was staring at the TV, trying to figure out how to record the college world series. Welcome to my Sunday morning.

James' hair laid like a rug, with a little help from a quart of water. Mike programmed the recorder and helped Henry find his shoes. Laces tied and Bibles in hand, the Guidry family piled into my Jeep Wrangler. No, it wasn't practical in my life. No, I didn't care what anyone thought.

We were off to church, and by living in a small town, we were only five minutes from the church parking lot. That logistical bonus made us only eight minutes late, which might have been a Guidry family record. When we lived in Dallas, we were routinely fifteen minutes late thanks to my husband and kids.

Oops-I'd forgotten small-town scrutiny. Everyone, whether Baptist or Methodist, clocked our late arrival. My herald into the community was not going well. Fortunately, the Melancons attended Graisseville Baptist Church.

We burst through the front door into the arms of Amy Melancon, the greeter. "Oh, look! It's the Guidry family! Welcome to our church! Let me take care of you!"

Oh, that Amy, she was the best! "James can go in the nursery—let me take you to drop him off."

Her husband Ken found Mike and Henry great spots in the same pew as Mike's parents, which made them happy. Ken reminded my husband about Children's Church. "It starts just before the pastor's sermon. Henry is the right age, and it's in your best interest to send him. You'll want to fully appreciate Brother Tom's sermon."

Amy directed me to the sanctuary after dropping off James, so I could enjoy the rest of the service with my family.

After church, Mike collected Henry and James while Amy introduced me to the women at Graisseville Baptist. Four invitations to lunch and two invitations to bridge! What was up with bridge in this town? I might learn the art of bridge at some point, but not yet. Lunch sounded fun, but bridge was definitely on pause.

My most prestigious invitation, to the Graisseville Ladies' Book Club, came from Eula Mae. At last, I met the artist of our unique painting!

"Of course! Yes, I'd love to be part of your book club. As a writer, I know the importance of reading both current and classic books. What book are you reading?"

"I'm sorry? Did you say you are a writer? I thought you stayed home with your children."

We faced each other, smiles like icy rivers curving upwards toward our foreheads. Oh Jen, did you step into yet another hornets' nest? Would I get brownie points for calling it a hornets' nest, an appropriate Southern term?

"Well, I don't write books, but I am a copywriter."

Eula Mae's friend, Anna Dunbar, wanted more information. "If you don't write books, sweetie, then what do you write?"

Deep breath Jen. Could I explain what I actually did without sounding like I did nothing? "I write the text for advertisements and other publicity material. That means I write content for a website, or a sales email, or really anything that needs words to sell stuff."

Eula Mae was the first to respond. "Oh! So you're in sales!"

Everyone else embraced that decision, and I should have been quiet. But oh no, I couldn't. I thought back to my communications degree and how my father-in-law found it useless. You're a writer, darn it! Graisseville defined my identity by my family tree. But I wanted to be defined by my career. A writer, not a salesperson.

"Actually, no, I'm a writer. I write the text that sells things. I don't think of myself as a salesperson. I think of myself as a writer." Good job Jen!

Ken Melancon spoke up. "Oh, hey! There are a couple of openings at the *Graisseville Gazette*! You should apply there! They need more writers, especially for the high school sports!"

Amy followed his lead. "Yes! Yes, that would be great! Also, I think that the editor of the *Gazette*, Hugh Cormier, has some connections with other papers. You know, Jen, this could be the start of some really good things!"

Cut your losses, Jen. Four invitations to lunch, two to bridge, and a coveted invitation to the Graisseville Ladies' Book Club. From a founding family member, no less.

"Now dear, we're reading Truman Capote's *Breakfast at Tiffany's.*"

"Oh wow! That's one of my all-time favorite reads. I've got a copy of the book from my college literature class, complete with detailed notes. I'll be ready!"

Eula Mae's icy river smile thawed just a little at my enthusiasm. "All right dear. Be sure and come prepared."

Bask in your invitations, go home and fix some peanut butter and honey sandwiches. Watch your husband doze by the light of the college world series and call it a day. This book club is right up your alley.

CHAPTER 6—THE BOOK CLUB THAT WASN'T

E ula Mae called me Monday morning, and I thanked her again for the invitation. "Should I bring anything? Brownies? A cake?"

"Oh, honey, don't go to any trouble! Just show up at my house on Wednesday at 10:00 a.m. If you're so inclined, please bring something light to munch on. It doesn't have to be homemade if you're not blessed in the kitchen. Just do your best."

The book club ladies were in for a treat! Ava spotted me two dozen chocolate *Petits Gateaux*, sure to woo the ladies' hearts. Honestly, I needed all the help I could get.

Petits Gateaux mean small cakes in French. The rich, creamy, and decadent desserts were very worthy of Eula Mae's circle of friends. Ava's treats had melted chocolate in the centers and were the stuff that dreams were made of.

I parked my Jeep Wrangler amongst the Volvos and Cadillacs and other luxury cars whose drivers probably didn't have small children. I was already feeling very out of place. But I had my *Petits Gateaux*, which looked pretty fancy, and I had my college degree from a respectable Southern university, even if it wasn't in Louisiana. I was going in.

Miss Founding Family Eula Mae Fontenot greeted me at the door and took my covered dish. She seemed pleased to see me as she ushered me into her home. I was literally speechless. The place was worthy of *Southern Living* magazine.

Right on time, or was I fifteen minutes late? The ladies were already chatting and eating. Eula Mae sat me down on a couch with more throw pillows than I owned bathroom towels. Juggling a couple on either side of me and one on my lap, I reached for a coffee cup. Was it a coffee cup? Yes, it had to be, just fancier than my World's Best Mom mug.

"Would you like some coffee, honey?" Anna Dunbar stood over me with an antique silver coffee server.

"Yes, ma'am, I would love some!" Don't sound too desperate, Jen!

Anna filled my cup a quarter of the way full.

Woman do you not understand the human need for caffeine?

What kind of bitter concoction had they disguised as coffee? In my urgency to get out of the house on time, I made sacrifices. I chose to spend time on my wardrobe rather than drink a cup of coffee. Honestly, I regretted that sacrifice. Next time, if there was a next time, it would be coffee over clothes.

"Mrs. Lila Trahan, I'd like you to meet Mrs. Jennifer Guidry. Granddaughter-in-law of Mrs. Evelyn Fontenot Guidry."

What? I was related by marriage to the Fontenot family? As Alice in Wonderland would say, curiouser and curiouser.

"Now that Jennifer is here," Eula Mae explained, "we can begin."

Seriously, Eula Mae? My watch read 10:02 a.m., literally two minutes past the start time! And what was with this Jennifer nonsense? Only my grandmother called me that. Sigh... Once again, the wrong place with the wrong people.

Eula Mae started the meeting. "Lila, would you tell us your thoughts on the book?"

Our president stood up, oh so elegant in her lavender dress. Was that silk? Please, Lord, don't let me spill anything on her!

"Ladies, I confess that I tried several times to read Chapter 1, but my mind was in another place. I have a situation that is concerning to me, and I'd like to discuss it."

Nods from the other ladies, so Lila continued. "Just the other day, I was driving by the park, and I saw Mack and Margie Taylor's daughter, Katie. And I am very sure she was with Rod Phillips' son, Matthew. They were kissing, but I think they were planning on doing more than that."

An outraged gasp from the circle. What did this have to do with the book?

The lack of good coffee caused my outburst, or so I rationalized. "Well, I have read this book several times, and I have to say I adore Holly Golightly! She is quirky, comical, and ultra-glamorous. She's fashionable and in the know, which I love." Glancing around for support, I saw a circle of frost.

Anna sat up straight and tall, looking over her glasses like my fifth-grade teacher Mrs. Phelps. "Ladies, I have to agree with Lila. I, too, am deeply concerned that our park is becoming a sort of hangout for teenage hooligans. I think that we should put aside our discussion of Mr. Capote's fine novel and put our heads together to solve this dilemma."

Take a breath, Jen. Yes, take another one. Maybe another sip of coffee? Ugh, never mind. What should I do? On one hand, my mother-in-law beamed with pride at my invitation to the book club. She'd never been asked, and I understood why. Ava Guidry was a lot of things, but she wasn't a gossip.

"I find Holly fascinating because she is also lonely and waiting to be rescued. If you look deeper than Holly's exterior, you can see the scared and lonely girl that she really is. She's terrified of being a caged animal but also tired of being alone." More frost, like a February morning after a cold snap.

Was this really a book club? Or was it an excuse to eat fancy desserts, drink bad coffee, and gossip?

Another breath. "Shouldn't concern over the park be addressed with the village government officials? Or the sheriff's department? I don't understand how our book club should be involved."

Anna peered over her glasses. "Jennifer, I don't believe you comprehend the secondary purpose of the Graisseville Ladies' Book Club. We began originally to meet and discuss books, but we soon realized there was a need in our community to guard and maintain the standards of our village founders. We still read and discuss various novels, of course, since that is our primary intent. But we also strive to identify potential problems in our community, intending to correct them so that we remain a morally sound village in this great state of Louisiana."

My armful of throw pillows and I sat quietly, anticipating our next move. Gossip was the worst way to spend my spare time. I was not a saint by any standards, but gossip was a cruel and ugly practice. No, I didn't want any part of a gossip club under the guise of keeping Graisseville fine and upstanding. But how to bow out gracefully? A glance at Eula Mae told me she had my back.

"Jennifer, I am sorry to say I may have miscommunicated how much time this book club would take from your schedule. I know that you are raising two fine young men, and you are also in sales. Perhaps our time constraints are too demanding on your family?"

Yet another sales dig. But on the flip side, I appreciated the out. Why such graciousness? Perhaps because we were distant cousins by marriage? At any rate, I was grateful that she gave me a way out the door.

"You know what, Eula Mae? I think you're right. I think I have too much on my plate right now. But I am forever grateful to the Graisseville Ladies' Book Club for welcoming me to your meeting today, and I hope to see you all soon." Sacrificing my *Petits Gateaux*, I turned tail and ran.

If Ava ever learned the whole story, she would have been proud of me. But was there anyone in the village like me? Where was my tribe, a group of people like me? God answered my question when Maggie walked into my life.

CHAPTER 7—MEETING MAGGIE

The end of July loomed in the horizon—I'd been in Louisiana since May! Henry started kindergarten in August, and I needed to register him. In my former life, we would be applying and interviewing and getting references since March. Ironically, when this whole let's-move-to-the-middle-of-nowhere adventure began. Back when I sat down with my husband to look over our magnitude of options and told me he couldn't breathe. It seemed so long ago, yet it had only been a few months. Time flies when your life has been turned upside down.

Here we were in East Baton Rouge Parish, a village of 298 people. We had literally two choices for Henry's school. Option One—pay for a boarding school in Switzerland or perhaps a place closer, like Baton Rouge. Those options were expensive and forced me to drive one hour each way to drop off and pick up my firstborn. Option Two was East Baton Rouge Parish School System. We didn't need to research and select Henry's school back in March. We all knew he was going to Homer E. Boudreaux Elementary.

The locals called it Homer E. or simply the Elementary School. I wasn't sure about sending my baby to this place, so Mike soothed my fears.

"Jen, I went to Homer E., and I turned out okay, didn't I? Okay, maybe don't answer that question specifically. But I did get into LSU, and that's not easy. I also got a great job in Dallas and met you, so this school system must be pretty good. Right? Right, Jen?"

I loved my husband but not for his persuasion skills. LSU, or Louisiana State University, was a fine university. I was not disagreeing with his statement, but should I bring up that his brother Joe let it slip a few years ago how Mike actually got into LSU? According to Joe, their cousin Beau, also known as the Honorable Beauregard Guidry, was the reason Mike was accepted into LSU. Well, Beau and his consistently substantial donations to the football program.

So, I said yes to Homer *E.* Boudreaux Elementary, which meant I would be standing in line at 8:00 a.m. on registration day along with all the other parents. Thank goodness I did, because that's where I met Maggie.

My coffee and I stood in line at Homer E. with the other kindergarten parents living within twenty miles, waiting for the doors to open. My head tipped back to let the last precious drops of coffee fall into my mouth. My heart grew heavy as I stared at my empty travel mug. What I wouldn't give for a cup of coffee.

A voice behind me whispered encouragement. "Don't worry, girl, I brought reinforcements."

My body swiveled towards the angel behind me, and I came face-to-face with a woman about my age and height. She reached into her wide-mouthed black-and-white striped bag and pulled out a thermos. My eyes bulged like grocery bags after a sale on hamburger meat. The angel opened the magical thermos, motioned to me, and began pouring as soon as my mug got close enough.

"Blessings upon you." My voice carried as much gratitude as I could muster at eight o'clock in the morning.

"Honey, I can tell this is your first kindergarten roundup. Next time, you'll be the one bringing coffee and snacks for the newbies."

Snacks? Did she say snacks? Could the woman read my mind? My angel put away her thermos of healing elixir and pulled out a blueberry muffin and a napkin. My hands opened like a morning flower, tears in my eyes. I'd met a kindred spirit, a member of my tribe.

"I'm Maggie Wheeler. I'd offer to shake your hand, but you'd have to put down either the muffin or the coffee. And we both know that won't happen." Her smile radiated sunshine. Perhaps my new hometown had potential.

"I'm Jen Guidry, and it's so nice to meet you."

Maggie chuckled. "It's nice to meet you, Jen Guidry, wife of Mike Guidry, owner of Big Ed's. Girl, I know who you are! I graduated two grades behind Mike. He used to come over to my house and play video games with my older brother, Charlie. Heck, I even went out with your brother-in-law Joe for a while back in high school. Gosh, that seems like a lifetime ago! Anyway, here I am, back in my hometown that I swore I'd never see again, married with two kids."

Oh my gosh, this woman was living my life!

"Last names, starting with the letters A through G, go to the second door on the right." Darn it, Mike, why didn't you have a name beginning with a letter farther down the alphabet?

Another smile of sunshine. "Don't worry, Jen, I know where to find you!" And just like that, my soul sister disappeared.

Why did registration take forever? After the longest fifteen minutes of my life, my feet carried me back to the hallway. Would my soul sister still be there? Alas, she'd vanished, like a rainbow after a thunderstorm. My heart dropped to my stomach—how would I find my coffee savior?

My Jeep pointed towards Big Ed's—maybe Mike could tell me more about my new best friend. As I pulled into the parking lot, my hope faded. Ugh—Mike had an end-of-summer sale on lawn care products. A packed parking lot meant no time for me. Who else? Ava! She had the kids anyway and loved to be helpful.

A plate of cane syrup cookies greeted me at the door. "Hello, Jenny! I'm hosting Mary Beth Miller's sister-in-law's cousin's baby shower this Saturday. Taste a cookie for me please—I tweaked the recipe a bit. What do you think?"

Was this woman determined to make me gain ten pounds before the end of the year? But I needed information, and that meant sacrifices.

"Mmmm, Ava, these are really good! You'll have to give me the recipe!" That was our standing joke. We both knew the only cookies I baked came from the refrigerated aisle of the grocery store.

Authentic cane syrup cookies are made with Louisiana's own Steen's cane syrup and lots of ginger. They can be soft and chewy or baked longer for a crispier texture. I preferred them crispy, and Ava did not disappoint. I continued with my conversation, mouth full.

"Oh, I met a really nice person this morning, Maggie Wheeler. We didn't exchange phone numbers though, so I wondered if you could help me with getting ahold of her. She shared her thermos of coffee and a blueberry muffin with me, and I want to thank her and maybe invite her to lunch." My heart swelled with hope—if anyone could help me, it would be my mother-in-law. Ava loved to be helpful, especially if it involved connecting people and information.

"Oh yes, Maggie Landry! She is one of the sweetest girls you'll ever meet! She's about your age too, isn't she? You know, she dated Joe for a while until she got tired of him spending all his time on the football field instead of with her. She is definitely the one that got away! Anyway, she went off to college, somewhere in Mississippi I think, on scholarship. Her parents said she met a nice young man named Wheeler, and they got married after graduation. They moved back here after her father passed away, so she could help out her mother."

One thing about Ava, she'd give you about ten minutes more information than you wanted. Walt always said if you ask Ava the time, she would tell you the life story of the man who sold her the watch. And you still wouldn't know the time. She also managed to sneak in a remark about Joe and his failed love life. I'd only met Joe a handful of times, but I could definitely see why he steered clear of his mom.

"Anyway, Ava, do you know how I can get a hold of Maggie? I'd really like to thank her for saving my sanity this morning."

Why was my mother-in-law headed to her cookbook collection? She pulled out a book and strolled toward me. Did she confuse phone numbers with pecan sandies? My mouth opened to protest, but I slammed it shut. Ava handed me a phone book, not a cookbook. Yet another small town convenience—phone books smaller than cookbooks, and families who still had landlines and published phone numbers. I flipped over to the W section and found five Wheelers.

"Ava, how do I know which one is Maggie's number?"

Was that a gust of wind blowing through the house? Oh no, just a sigh from my mother-in-law, signaling her irritation. "It's the only one on Pecan Street. The other Wheelers are all kin, and they live on the far side of town, over by the dairy farm. The Wheeler dairy farm."

Why, yes, Ava, of course. Everyone knew that. Everyone except me. My turn to imitate a gust of wind in the kitchen.

"Boys, let's go! Thank you again for Maggie's number, Ava. No, we really don't need any more cookies—we still have the chocolate-covered pecans from three days ago."

After watching television all morning, Henry and James needed to run. "Why don't you two go outside? Mom will be out soon after I make a cup of coffee."

Mike didn't drink coffee, so one of our marital tools was my single-serve French coffee press. My husband didn't complain about wasted coffee, and I always had a fresh cup when needed. As I watched my coffee brew, my cell phone rang. An unknown caller—could it be my coffee angel? Take a chance, Jen, and answer the call!

"Hey, Jen, it's Maggie Wheeler. I told you I know where to find you!"

My heart skipped a beat, like in high school when the popular girl says *hi*. In my case, the popular girl was calling. She was calling me! Act casual, Jen. You have such a busy and fulfilled life—no big thing for Maggie Wheeler to call.

"Hi, Maggie, how are you? I'm glad you called! I wanted to thank you again for the lifesaving coffee and muffin." Dial down the enthusiasm Jen!

"Oh yeah, no problem. My daughter, Maya, is my second turn at the roundup, so I knew what to bring. When I did it a few years ago with my firstborn, Tessa, I didn't bring any coffee or snacks. Let's just say the people around me were as sorry as I was. I was impressed that you thought to bring a full mug of coffee, though!"

Oh, I really liked this woman!

"Anyway, Jen, I wanted to see if you were free for lunch this Saturday. I thought we'd jump right in with a playdate. You can bring your kids over to play at our house, I'll feed them chicken nuggets and juice boxes, and we can have something a little more grown-up. Maybe chicken salad and iced tea? I know Mike has to work on Saturdays, and I can send my husband fishing for the day. He'll be so grateful for my generosity that I can probably leverage that for a future home project."

Maggie's laugh reminded me of Saturday morning breakfast at my grandmother's house. We always felt full and satisfied—and happy. Maggie's laugh gave me those same feelings. She probably laughed a lot. Happy people have a positive outlook on life, and Maggie was one of those people. It's easy for me to whine and complain instead of counting my blessings. To stay positive, I'd learned to surround myself with positive people. Maggie was someone who could fulfill that role nicely.

"Count us in!" My mind imagined Maggie pulling the phone from her ear. Dial it down, Jen! "What time should we be there?"

"In for a penny, in for a pound, as my grandmother used to say. Let's do 10:00 a.m., which would give us plenty of time for coffee and chat before lunch."

My heart protested as we said our goodbyes. Saturday was so far away! My coffee and I drifted to the couch, letting it all sink in. The phone call, the invitation, the potential of a good friend. My heart leaped for joy, singing a show tune. My mouth turned upwards, possibly permanently. Then reality set in, as my thoughts turned to the playdate.

What should I wear? What if the kids don't get along? What if Henry called one of Maggie's daughters a *poophead*, as he'd been doing lately? What if James threw a hissy fit like the one two days before? Should I call back and cancel?

Calm down, Jen, just breathe. This was the first person I'd met with a real connection. Yes, everyone had been super nice, but Maggie was the first to get me. This playdate was crucial for my emotional well-being. If my kids acted like, well, my kids, then I would deal with it. My heart slowed and my breathing followed. Time to go outside and wrangle the children. As I took a step my foot wobbled. What was that under my toes? The small metal car brought me back to my life. My Zen moment was over.

"All right, boys! Show me how many times you can go down the slide in a minute. Go!" Balancing the all-important mug of sanity, I opened the door and rejoined reality.

Later, I saw a text from Ava. "Did Maggie call you? She asked for your number, and I thought it would be okay to give it to her. I hope I didn't overstep any boundaries. Please advise." Thank you, God, for my amazing mother-in-law!

CHAPTER 8—THE ALMOST DISASTROUS PLAYDATE

Mike will never know, but I spent more time choosing an outfit for that playdate than I ever did for him. After twelve clothing changes, I went with casual yet stylish. At least, I hoped so. A pair of jeans with no holes and a lavender T-shirt with no stains. A silver necklace, a matching pair of earrings, and my favorite sandals kicked it up a notch. To up the style, I dug around under the bathroom sink, found my curling iron, and spruced up my hair a bit. This was an important day!

I dressed the boys in denim shorts and tennis shoes since they'd be playing outside. Henry insisted on wearing the "I'm a country boy" shirt his grandfather gave him, which irritated me. But I didn't push the issue. James, at three years old, still wore what I chose, so he looked pretty cute in his dark-green shirt with dinosaurs.

Balanced by my purse sat Ava's browned butter oatmeal cookies. She was almost as excited about my blossoming friendship as I was. "Maggie could be your first real friend! Honey, I'm so excited." Maybe a little too excited.

Mike was even more excited—he knew how much I missed my girlfriends back in Dallas. My happiness increased his happiness, and he knew that would take at least one local friend.

Arriving at Maggie's house on Pecan Street made me think of the other four Wheelers. How could I know Maggie wasn't one of them? Would I ever get the nuances and backstories that everyone else in town took for granted? Maybe Maggie could be my tour guide on that journey. A knock on the door produced a wide-eyed curly-haired girl about eight years old. Most likely Maggie's oldest Tessa.

"Good morning! You must be Tessa. I'm Mrs. Guidry, and this is Henry, and this is James." Did my smile show more confidence than I was feeling? Hopefully.

"Mom! They're here!" Tessa bellowed toward the room behind her. She turned back in my direction. "My mom said to let you in because she's trying to find a clean pair of jeans that still fit good."

Tessa opened the door and ushered us in. "I don't particularly like boys, but my mom says I have to play with yours for at least an hour. Then I can pretend I don't feel well and go to my room."

Should I laugh or nod my head? Maybe both. "Well, Tessa, I appreciate your honesty. Would you take these cookies into the kitchen?"

Tessa inspected the plate with a critical eye. "Are these oatmeal cookies?"

Honesty should be repaid with honesty. "Yes, they're oatmeal with chocolate chips." Score! A smile from Tessa, the first one. Point for Team Guidry!

"I hate the ones with raisins—they're yucky. So I'm glad you used chocolate chips." She carried them confidently into the kitchen just as Maya appeared with a football.

"Let's go play! I'm the quarterback, and you're the wide receiver." A quick appraisal of James' football skills. "You can be the linebacker. Let's go!"

My boys were too afraid to question Maya but excited to go outside and run around. They didn't know a wide receiver from a linebacker, but Maya was going to whip them into shape.

Maggie appeared, in a clean pair of jeans that fit. "Welcome to our humble home! Coffee?"

Not waiting for an answer, she turned and headed for the kitchen. I trailed after her, like a puppy dog. Heck, I would follow that woman anywhere with the promise of coffee.

Before the first sip hit my taste buds, James fell into my arms with tears streaming down his face. Maya and Henry were right behind him, scowling.

"Mom, this kid can't tackle. I'd bench him, but you didn't give me a deep enough bench!" Wow! That girl and my husband needed to get together. He'd appreciate having someone intelligent to share football strategies.

Maggie's lips snapped into a straight line, and her face flushed. "Maya, give him a break! He's only three years old!"

Face still flushed and eyes tearing up, Maggie pleaded. "Jen, I am so sorry! Greg has been teaching Maya all about football, and I'm afraid she's obsessed with it at the moment."

Tessa appeared out of thin air. "It's okay, Mom, I'll take him into my room and we'll read some books." Thank you, Ava, for those browned butter oatmeal cookies! And thank you for using chocolate chips. Those baked goods impressed Tessa and rescued my son from a humiliating football career at age three.

As payment, Tessa took six cookies off the plate and handed one to James. Hard to eat a cookie while crying, so the waterworks disappeared. Free hands clasped together, the pair headed off.

"Just another day in the paradise we call motherhood, right, Maggie?" My smile reflected relief as I took my first sip of coffee.

Maggie grabbed my arm. "Just promise me that my children won't ruin our friendship, okay?"

She looked at me hopefully. Oh my gosh, this woman was serious! And I was terrified my children would wreck everything.

"Umm, Maggie, I should probably confess right now that I have terrible children as well. In fact, Henry is going through a phase right now where he calls everyone a *poophead*. Also, when I picked him up from Sunday School last week, his teacher pulled me aside. My child informed the class that angels have wings and booties. And they poop and pee, just like we do. Believe me when I tell you my kids are not perfect by any standard."

Maggie's eyes scanned my face, then she burst out laughing. "Okay, let's spend a few minutes confessing how bad our kids are and how horrible we are at parenting them."

An hour and a half and many cups of coffee later, we were still detailing our imperfect children. We also confessed our failed attempts at making them perfect. There were interruptions for drinks and bathroom trips (for adults and children), but no more tears or issues. We finally stopped our confessions at eleven thirty when the kids trickled into the living room asking for lunch.

Henry and James declared Maggie's chicken nuggets and juice boxes the best they'd ever sampled, and I thought the same about my chicken salad and iced tea. Food with friends makes the food taste even better.

As our playdate wound down, I scrambled to get some necessary information. Maggie's husband, Greg had just scored a full-time job with potential tenure at LSU in Baton Rouge. Maggie worked at the bank in Zachary, so she had to be using some sort of childcare. Reliable daily childcare was critical. My projects were consistently late and not as good as they used to be. I wasn't bringing my A-game to work, and my boss confirmed it.

"Jen, I've cut you some slack because of the move and everything. But there's no more slack. You need to find childcare or another job." I loved my job, so I chose the childcare option.

Maggie and I cleared the table, a perfect time to ask my question. "Before we end our playdate, I need to ask you about childcare. I can't find anyone to watch the boys. And my mother-in-law has also been asking, but she's not having any luck either. Do you have any suggestions?"

Maggie's eyes twinkled. "Well, I know someone. She's kept both my kids since they were babies. Now officially she doesn't have any openings, because she likes brand-new parents with babies, so she can train the whole family. But I will talk to her and explain the situation, and I'm sure she'll take your kids."

This woman was my hero and I threw my arms around her.

Maggie laughed, and once again I was at my grandmother's house on a Saturday morning. "Jen, I know how you feel. It's hard to move somewhere new and find just the right person to keep your babies. You will love Darla, though. She's wonderful! I'll give her a call Monday morning and then I can text her information to you. Just let me pave the way first."

Soon it was time to wrangle the boys and say our goodbyes. Ava's miracle cookies had disappeared and I scooped up the plate. My purse was bulging with a bag of gourmet coffee from New Orleans, a gift from Maggie.

As we headed out the door, Maggie said something that changed my life. She kept her voice low and steady, so it didn't register. As I walked down the steps, yelling at boys to slow down, her comment sank in. For the second time that week, I had hope. Maybe I could enjoy living in Graisseville.

"Greg and I are thinking about opening a coffee shop in Downtown Graisseville. Don't give me your opinion right now—just think about it. We can discuss it next time we get together. I'd love to know your thoughts on the matter."

CHAPTER 9-MAGGIE'S NEW ADVENTURE

M aggie called me on Monday with a bounty of good news. Based on her glowing recommendation, Henry and James could start at daycare the next day. She hadn't mentioned Henry's fondness for calling people *poopheads* or James' delight in throwing tantrums. Henry could also go to after-school care when he started kindergarten the next month. Darla's prices were reasonable, and I could earn enough to cover the cost with my windfall of time during the day. I would be writing copy instead of debating which Power Ranger was the best and who didn't flush the toilet.

Maggie's other news made my heart flutter.

"I really owe you, for speaking to Darla. My boss was about to fire me."

"My pleasure really, and it'll give our kids more time together."

"True! Okay, now you've got to tell me! Are you and Greg seriously thinking about opening a coffee shop?" Please Lord, please let Maggie be serious about this venture. I pray she wasn't over caffeinated and exaggerated.

"Well, I'm extremely serious. Greg, of course, is concerned about the finances. He'll be making a lot more at LSU than *E* Burp, so I think we will be fine. He's also concerned coffee shops are usually open nights and weekends, which is when we spend our time together as a family and as a couple. He's worried our marriage may suffer, and we won't see our kids as often."

All true, but not helping my need for a local coffee shop.

"On the other hand, I truly hate my job at the bank! I want to use my business degree for something other than processing loan applications and playing mom to the twenty-somethings the bank keeps hiring. If I'm going to make coffee every morning and every afternoon, I want it to be good coffee, and I want it to be for people who appreciate it."

Maggie and I spent the next hour working through all the concerns. She wanted me to help her decide the coffee shop was a good idea, and I was up for the task. At the end of our call, she was going to talk to the bank about a loan. She would also speak with the mayor about leasing some space downtown.

"If I had some hard numbers for us to review, it would make our decision easier."

That night I dreamed about coffee shops and espresso shots and woke up ready to produce a full day's work.

After getting Henry and James settled in at Darla's, I sat in front of the computer to churn out some stellar copy content. Questions crowded my mind. What should we name the coffee shop? What about the theme and decor? I jotted down ideas and Googled word strings such as "best coffee shop names," "favorite coffee shop drinks," and "ten best things to sell in a coffee shop." I broke for lunch and texted Maggie, wondering if she'd made any progress on her decision.

"Hey, girl! How's your day?"

No response-she was probably in the break room, making more coffee for the twenty-somethings.

After a lunch of leftovers, I began my newest project. When I was on the clock for my boss, I put my phone on silent and turned it over, so I couldn't see the screen. I used the Emergency Bypass On feature only for certain people. The bypass feature meant that only Mike, Ava, and Walt, and my parents' calls would ring through my phone. All other calls went to voicemail, so I could work undisturbed. I activated the bypass feature for Darla's number, making her one of the chosen ones.

I kept my focus and typed tirelessly until five o'clock, then rewarded myself by checking my phone screen. Maggie had blown up my phone for the last few hours:

How's my day? It's freakin' awesome!!!!!!

Aren't you going to ask me why?

C'mon! Ask me why!

Jen, you there?

Are you kidding me????

You've got to be kidding me!

Next were the multiple missed calls, one every two minutes in a fifteen-minute time span. Then more texting, with a flood of coffee cups and smiley emojis. Last, just two words, all in capital letters: Call me.

"Oh my gosh! Where have you been? You've got to get over here! It's amazing. It's just truly amazing!" Had the woman taken a breath? Wait, there it was! Jump in, Jen!

"Where are you? I'll be right there, but I've got to pick up the boys."

Maggie didn't skip a beat. "Darla can keep them until 6:00 p.m. You've got to get over here now!"

"Okay, but where are you?"

"Downtown, you've got to get downtown right now, Jen!" In a town of 298 residents, downtown was easy to find and so was parking. Keys in hand I headed out the door. Halfway down the road, I realized I'd forgotten to lock my front door. Small towns have a ridiculously low crime rate. Hopefully, that would continue to hold true for the next few hours.

Maggie's Suburban sat in front of a vacant building, so I parked beside it. Although I couldn't see Maggie, I heard her through the open door.

"And we'll put three tables here, and in that corner will be a small stage for acoustic guitar players and singers. We can put some really comfy couches over here and a bookshelf with books and board games." Maggie paused to breathe and spun around, spying my look of confusion.

I was never sure what unbridled enthusiasm was until I saw my friend sprinting toward me. It was a wild horse galloping at full speed with no intention of slowing down.

Throwing herself into my arms she screamed. "Oh my gosh! It's just so exciting! I wanted you to be here with me! Where have you been? We signed the lease and applied for the bank loan! Now, the lease is contingent upon the loan, but everyone feels confident it will go through in a few weeks, hopefully by the middle of August. Just in time for both my girls to be in school, and I will have the time I need to get this place up and running. Oh, Jen, isn't this just the best!"

Maggie's hug cut off my air supply, making it difficult to respond. Did it even matter? Nothing I said would have made any difference. Maggie finally let go of me and led me over to a tall man dressed in khakis and sporting professor—looking glasses. Greg Wheeler, I presume?

"Oh honey, I want you to meet my new best friend. Jen, this is my husband Greg. Isn't this so exciting?" Maggie ran off to take some pictures on her phone.

Time for small talk. "Well, isn't this exciting? I'm glad to meet you, especially on the first day of your new business venture."

Greg stared at me through professor glasses, then took the hand I had offered. "So you're Jen. Maggie says you're the one that walked her through the last steps to quit her job and open this place."

Hmmm...perhaps Greg didn't share Maggie's business-owner excitement.

Greg looked deep into my eyes. "I just want to thank you so much. I was trying to be the voice of reason. But last night, I realized that sometimes reason has to take a back seat to happiness. You gave Maggie the courage to take this leap of faith, and she sold me on your plan. I think this venture will be successful and make my wife excited to go to work again. Thanks to you, Jen, my wife is truly happy." The man released my hand and walked over to his wife.

My confidence soared! I'd just helped my friend find happiness. And I would have a coffee shop minutes from my front door. Just a month so back, I was distraught to give up a source of coffee on virtually every corner. Flash forward to my current situation where I had a best friend who owned a coffee shop. My gaze wandered to the horizon, embracing my idyllic situation.

"Hey, Jen! I'd like you to meet Ruby Bergeron, our village mayor. Ruby, this is Jen Guidry."

Ruby smiled and held out her hand. Our mayor's cool green eyes and square jaw told me she was a woman used to getting her way.

"Nice to meet you, Jen. Now, Maggie, remember that the village owns this space, and as such, we have the final say on the décor, the furnishings, and all food and drink items sold. So don't go putting anything in here without talking to me."

Maggie nodded like an obedient child, but did she realize exactly what that meant? Ruby could make or break this business. Was this such a good idea after all?

Ruby and Maggie saw eye to eye on the decor and the furnishings. Ruby liked the idea of musicians playing quietly in the corner and creating an "air of civility" as long as they didn't disturb the other tenants. We all agreed musicians playing without amps would be quiet enough. Ruby and Maggie definitely didn't see eye to eye on the menu items, though. Our mayor wanted everything low calorie and low fat, because of her ongoing mission to make Graisseville the healthiest village in Louisiana. She'd made a promise.

Four families claimed credit as the first residents of Graisseville. There were several stories how the village was named, but the official one was my favorite. The families were on the verge of starvation, so Joseph Fontenot and Louis Hebert vowed not to return without enough food for everyone. They returned with three wild hogs, each weighing approximately two hundred pounds. The four families feasted on the hogs and survived until spring.

Louisiana was originally owned by France, so there are many locations in the state with French names. Baton Rouge is French for "Red Stick" while Lafayette was named after a French pirate. Towns are also called villages.

When the families named the village, the men wanted Porcs Gras (POOR-GRAW), which literally means "fat hogs" in French. The women were horrified, and there were many heated arguments between the two factions for several weeks. The families finally reached a compromise and agreed upon the name *Graisse Village*, which means "Fat Village."

The proper French grammar for "Fat Village" is "Gros Village" (GROW-VEE-LODGE), but the female founders thought the French word *"gros"* was, well, gross. They used the feminine version of *graisse* (GRACE), thinking that version seemed more elegant. Through the years, Graisse Village was shortened to Graisseville, for better or worse.

Ruby was an Hebert by birth and a Bergeron by marriage, and both sets of ancestors were founding family members. The story goes that the Heberts never voted for either of the names Fat Hogs or Fat Village. They petitioned for Belle Bayou (BELL-BYE-YOU) after a creek that runs near the village. Belle Bayou, which means beautiful creek, was a lovely name for a place the founders also called home.

At one point, the Hebert family circulated a petition to change the village name from Graisseville to Belle Bayou. When residents were told how much it would cost to change the name on everything, they told the Heberts to stop being sore losers and find another movement to champion.

When Ruby ran for mayor, she went in a different direction. Her campaign platform "Our name means fat, but we aren't" was a disastrous slogan, but she ran unopposed. The mayor's job involved a ridiculous amount of work for only $23 a month, and no one else wanted the position. It didn't hurt she had two founding family names, which meant the other families voted for her. Those people bonded together over fat hogs many winters ago, and the loyalty had been passed on through the generations. Fortunately for

Mike, the Dairy Delight and the Gas 'n' More had been in business before Ruby took office. Both places brought in enough revenue that no one would force them to limit their menus. That brought us to the mayor in the coffee shop threatening to restrict Maggie's menu.

My friend wanted to sell drinks like other coffee shops—mocha frappe, caramel cappuccino, and café con leche. Ruby had her grandson research the calorie and fat content of the proposed drink menu and was less than pleased with the results. She insisted on an emergency meeting of the village council the following Saturday morning. The only item on the agenda was a discussion of the unacceptable drink choices.

Maggie and I invested several hours trying to plan a convincing argument for her menu, but we knew it was a losing battle. There was no way Maggie was ever going to sell the high-calorie and fat coffee concoctions, much less the cinnamon rolls and boudin kolaches she wanted to offer.

The meeting was short and to the point.

"Maggie, this is unacceptable, simply unacceptable. If you recall, my campaign platform was *Our name means fat, but we aren't*. The people agreed with me as evidenced by my landslide win. We don't want these unhealthy drinks served in our village."

The rest of the village council consisted of a sheriff's deputy and the Board of Aldermen, who all remained silent. If Maggie wanted to serve her drinks, she would have to move on to the next step. She would have to present her case to the Board of Aldermen and ask them to amend the law.

In our village, the Board of Aldermen was the legislative body that created, passed, and amended local laws. They also approved the annual village budget. Maggie felt pretty confident the Aldermen would side with Ruby since they had remained silent in the council meeting. She had no choice but to agree to serve drinks and food items under three hundred calories.

My friend was almost in tears when she called me after the meeting. "I just don't know what to do, Jen, I really don't. How is the shop going to succeed if I'm limited to three hundred calories per item? Ruby may even limit each order to five hundred calories total or less. I need to talk to Greg, but I think I've made a huge mistake."

We chatted for a few minutes as I tried to console her, but Maggie was beyond defeated. "Oh, let me let you go. Charlie's calling me." Charlie was Maggie's brother, a buddy of Mike's from high school, and one of the best contractors in town. If he couldn't do the job, he knew a guy who could. Charlie was the general contractor for our barn renovation, but he had managed to work on the coffee shop rehab on the weekends for his little sister. He was working at the coffee shop that fateful Saturday morning when he beeped into our call.

Maggie phoned me back almost immediately. "Jen, come down to the coffee shop! Charlie wants to show us something. Don't bring anyone, not even the boys. It's a secret and I don't want anyone to know."

"Ooh, I love secrets! I'll call my weekend go-to sitter."

Ava and Walt were delighted to babysit, and Walt picked up the boys on his way to get pizza from Graisseville Gas 'n' More. I had the best in-laws ever!

Couldn't my Jeep go any faster? I parked right in front and jumped out, almost tripping over my feet. As I caught my breath, I stepped inside the building and spotted Maggie and Charlie.

"Hey, Jen. Now that you're here, we can get started. Ladies, you won't believe me, so I am just going to show you," Charlie stepped inside the beginnings of a bathroom. We obediently followed and circled around the tiny space.

"As Maggie knows, this space has been vacant for many years. The village has tried unsuccessfully to rent it out, but Maggie's been the first to sign a lease. There is no bathroom in this building, and according to the building code, we have to put one in. Maggie and I decided to put it towards the back, where the pipes from the building next door are located. Imagine my surprise when I was knocking on the wall, trying to find the pipes, and found this instead." Charlie pushed on a section of the wall, and it opened like a door.

Twin gasps as Charlie took a flashlight and shone it inside. "I could be totally off base on this, but, ladies, I think we've discovered a speakeasy from the Prohibition era."

The Eighteenth Amendment of the United States Constitution took effect in January 1920 and lasted until 1933. The amendment prohibited the manufacture, transportation, and sale of alcoholic beverages, which gave people the opportunity to create illegal revenue streams. Specifically, moonshiners thrived, and business owners built secret bars and clubs called speakeasies. Charlie believed we had stumbled upon such a secret bar. I was captivated by the history sitting before me, but the wheels inside Maggie's head were turning.

"You know, this speakeasy gave people a chance to enjoy themselves without the eyes of the government looking down on them. Maybe it's time for this piece of history to come out of retirement."

We swore each other to secrecy and devised a plan that was extremely devious and only slightly illegal.

CHAPTER 10—THE SECRET COFFEE ROOM

M aggie and I went round and round, trying to come up with a cute and clever name for the coffee shop. A name that brought in both the high school students and the oilfield workers. The church ladies, but also the motorcycle club. Not so clever that people didn't know what she sold. We played with the name "Maggie's Coffee 'n' More," a take on Big Ed's Parts 'n' More and Graisseville Gas 'n' More. In the end, we kept coming back to Maggie's Coffee Shop. It was simple and easy to remember, and the Louisiana secretary of state said there was no other business with that name.

Charlie made good on his promise and the shop opened on Labor Day weekend. Maggie's kids and Henry had been in school for a week, James was thriving at Darla's, and I had been meeting or exceeding all my project deadlines. My boss was off my back, Maggie was on cloud nine with her new business venture, and life was good. We just needed to nail down all the details of the secret coffee room. I did some research on speakeasies, thinking that what was good for Prohibition would probably work for us. Google and Wikipedia did not disappoint.

The term speakeasy most likely came from the phrase "speak easy," as in patrons had to speak easy or whisper a password through a small opening in a door to gain access. Many times, the password was a person's name, as in "Jen Guidry," which meant "Jen Guidry sent me." It all sounded so clandestine, like the *Mission Impossible* movies. In reality, we were breaking the law, and Maggie's husband, Greg, was not excited about the plan.

"Maggie, I just don't think this is a good idea. If you get found out, and you will, you are going to be on the wrong side of the law. Ruby Bergeron could shut down your coffee shop, and she is not someone you want to make angry. I really wish you wouldn't do this."

"Oh, honey! Ruby's not going to shut down the only source of revenue that space in twelve years!"

"I hope you're right, and the bank does too. If this business fails, we can't pay our loan."

After much discussion, we started with Maggie's family. They wanted to support their girl and enjoyed a good cinnamon roll. The name Landry was not one of the four founding families, so they felt no particular loyalty to Ruby. We left out her cousin, Chris Landry. Being a parish deputy, we didn't want him to choose between badge and blood. Maggie would be running the coffee house all by herself at first. There would be no one on the other side of the secret door to verify a password and welcome fellow lawbreakers. We used the secret coffee room to stock baked goods and stored all the sugary syrups, whipped cream, and other drink additions up front. We kept the contraband in bottles with red labels.

Maggie stocked the sugar-free syrups and skim milk in containers with black labels.

Customers not concerned about calories (or breaking the law) would begin the order process with the words "Charlie sent me." Maggie knew to give the customer all the high-calorie goodness she could fit in those drinks. After the customer had paid for and received the contraband drink order, he or she could then go to the secret room for illegal food items. Once in the bathroom, the patron would push the section of the wall just under the sign, "Wash your hands like you just ate crawfish and you have to put in your contacts."

The door to the secret coffee room would open, and the customer could enter and purchase assorted baked goods on the honor system. Maggie's brother, Charlie, was honored that his name was the password.

After two weeks, Maggie was making a lot more from her covert customers than her honest ones. Sugar-free and fat-free drinks had a higher cost than unhealthy ones because let's face it, it's more expensive to eat better. Most people didn't want the healthier versions, anyway. Her illegal drinks were a big chunk of her profit margin, but she was also making a killing from the banned baked goods.

"Jen, I feel horrible because I'm not paying sales tax on the food. But I would have to ring them up on the register to include them in my sales, and that's just too risky."

"Agreed! Let's schedule another playdate soon to put our heads together. We'll find a solution."

We kept our word on the playdate but couldn't come up with a plan. How could we include the backroom bakery without alerting Ruby and the Aldermen? We kept things status quo and prayed a solution would present itself. Our patience was rewarded.

After a month, Maggie was able to hire some of her relatives, and they could be trusted to keep the Secret Coffee Room, well, a secret. Maggie purchased a computer screen, refrigerator, and a coffee machine for the secret room and put a staff person back there to run it. She devised a system so customers could order in the front and pick up in the back. Maggie rang up healthy drink orders up front, such as cold brew with nonfat milk and black coffee with artificial sweetener. She also rang up food items like fruit, yogurt, and cottage cheese. When the customer gave her the magic words, Maggie would flag the order as SCR, or Secret Coffee Room, and the employee in the backroom would see it on the computer screen. The employee would fill the order using a software program created by Maggie's cousin. The program took the order and converted it to the actual menu items. Cold brew with nonfat milk and a cup of yogurt was actually iced coffee with cream and vanilla syrup and a cinnamon roll. After Maggie took payment, the customer entered the Secret Coffee Room to pick up the order.

Maggie slept more soundly because she was reporting all her sales and paying taxes. We had been concerned about law-abiding citizens entering the coffee shop and actually wanting yogurt or fruit. Maggie found that virtually all her customers wanted the good stuff, the contraband. Her cousin, Deputy Landry, came by almost weekly and ordered plain black coffee. Everyone else used the password. Maggie relaxed as the coffee shop showed a profit. Soon, her regulars asked if they could move the tables and chairs from the coffee shop to the secret room. They wanted to sit and enjoy their purchases. Maggie obliged, although the coffee shop looked sad and lonely.

"Miss Maggie, could I bring my dominos so we can play a few games after finishing their breakfast? We'll be as quiet as mice." How could Maggie say no?

One day in early November, about two months after the shop opened, Ruby stopped by to order some unsweet tea (almost unheard of in the South) and to visit.

"Well, Maggie, I want to tell you I am just so pleased with your menu! Why you even have the calorie content listed beside each menu item."

"Yes, Mayor, just like it says in my lease agreement."

"But I am sorry to see that your shop appears a little vacant. Maybe if you put in some tables and chairs, you'd have more customers. I do hope you understand the absence of patrons does not mean your rent can be late. Have a good day!" Ruby paid for her tea and left.

Maggie grabbed her cell phone as Ruby exited the premises. I had added the Emergency Bypass On feature for Maggie's number so that her calls would also ring through to my phone. Maggie needed to vent, and I got an earful about that visit.

A week later, I stopped by the coffee shop and chatted with my friend. I had the boys in tow, so we ordered some healthy milk and black coffee. Maggie didn't actually have any healthy food on the premises, so I brought my own snacks.

"Hey, girl! How's your morning?"

"Well, Greg's pretty happy with the small profit we're turning. But this is not the coffee shop you and I conjured up in our heads. I'd love to have an acoustic guitar in here, but who's going to play to an empty shop? I want to sit and chat with my customers, but they're all in the secret coffee room. I just don't know what to do."

Poor Maggie! What could I say to make her feel better?

Ruby pushed open the door, and the jangle of the bell brought us to attention. Without thinking, we both stood at attention, ready for inspection.

"Well, hello, Jen, how are you? Hello, Maggie. I see business hasn't picked up since I was last here." Ruby scanned the room with a frown. "Did you think about my suggestion? Adding some tables and chairs?" She stared at Maggie, the corners of her mouth diving down in displeasure.

"Actually, I did think about it, Ruby. But most people take their orders to go. So I'm not sure the seating would be an improvement."

Whew, good answer, Maggie!

"Well, I had an idea for your little shop. You mentioned you wanted to bring in some musicians to entertain patrons. It just so happens that my nephew, Dillon, has graduated EBurp with a degree in music, and he is available to perform for as many evenings as you would like. Since you are a friend of mine, he offered to only charge you $100 per hour with a two-hour minimum."

How was that a favor for Maggie? The nephew definitely, but not Maggie.

My friend hesitated, not sure how to respond in a kindly way. Gather your thoughts girl! "Ruby, I appreciate your consideration, I really do. I just don't think I can afford your nephew at this time."

Ruby's smile grew wider. "Don't be silly, Maggie! I've seen your numbers from the sales tax reports. You are doing very well with your new business. But just think how much better you could be doing with a professional musician playing in your shop!"

So now he was a professional musician?

Save your friend Jen! "Maggie, shouldn't you talk over something like this with your husband? I mean, he is part owner of the coffee shop."

Relief spilled over my friend's face like a quick morning rain. We would need some time to put our heads together and find a way out of this mess.

"Very well, Maggie, but get back to me as soon as possible. Dillon is extremely popular, and I don't know how long he'll be available. As I said, he's doing this as a favor to me because you're my friend."

How did Ruby rationalize that statement--Maggie being her friend? The two women hadn't spoken regularly until Maggie opened the coffee shop. Friend must be a relative term for our mayor.

As Ruby exited, Alderman Clay Terry entered. Poor Maggie! She had all the signs of hyperventilating. First the mayor, then an alderman darkening the doorstep of her illegal establishment. And on the same day! That was enough to make anyone stressed.

"Hello, Maggie, I hope you're doing well today." Clay inclined his head at Graisseville's newest business owner. Then he turned his sights on me. "I don't believe I've had the pleasure of your acquaintance. My name is Clay Terry, and I went to school with your father-in-law. He is one of my dearest friends." He offered his hand, and I shook it.

By now I'd learned most everyone knew who I was. Those introductions didn't surprise me anymore.

His head swiveled back to the counter. "Maggie, I'd like to speak with you in private. Is this a good time?"

Was Maggie going to faint or throw up first? Hard to tell. "Clay, anything you want to say to me, you can say to Jen."

Oh, thank goodness! This girl didn't want to miss a thing! Had we been busted? Was he shutting down the coffee shop? Could Walt step in and stop it since he and Clay were friends? Would the boys stay quiet long enough for me to get answers to all these questions?

"All right then, I'll get to the point. It has come to my attention that your lease does not allow items over three hundred calories to be sold in your lease space. It has also come to my attention that people like Bubba Gladney and Moe Gladstone and the crew from the

Gas 'n' More are walking around the village drinking out of coffee cups with the words *Maggie's Coffee Shop* on them. I feel very confident these men would never darken the doorstep of a place that sells sugar-free coffee drinks and yogurt and cottage cheese."

Clay clenched his jawline, but his eyes twinkled. "I have been reviewing your sales reports from the state, and you are generating some significant revenue for a new business. And Graisseville is benefitting from your new business. There are several of us on the Board of Aldermen who want to see you continue to succeed. We understand that when businesses are profitable, the entire community benefits. I would like to find a way for everything in the coffee shop to take place in the lease's front space, rather than in the back." Yes, definitely a smile on Clay's face.

I stood back and listened intently, feeding my boys snacks to ensure silence. Maggie and Clay spoke for about fifteen minutes and devised a plan. Clay would propose to the Board of Aldermen that Maggie receive special permission to sell food and drink items of her choice as long as she met state health regulations.

"You'll have the board's support, and we'll deal with the wrath of Ruby. In return, could you please add cruller donuts to the menu? They're my wife's favorites."

Such a small price to pay! "Wait until the board meets next week before making all the changes. I'll let you know when you're officially approved. Then you can sell all the food and drinks you want."

As he walked out the door, he glanced over his shoulder. "Oh, and keep that secret room available. I have some ideas." The alderman didn't miss a stride as he walked out the door.

CHAPTER 11—HANGING WITH HUGH

Navigating and processing the small-town charm and eccentricities exhausted me. Most days, I had the hang of it. But some days not so much. The day I paid our water bill was a day I had it all figured out.

The water system board maintained our village water. We didn't have a water tower, just a water tank. Standing twenty feet high and absent a logo, it was practical and served its purpose. About twelve feet from the water tank was a brown plastic mailbox to slip in payments. Most people stopped by the Graisseville *Gazette* instead. They paid their bill, chatted with the editor, and got the inside scoop it hit the weekly paper. Hugh Cormier was a colorful storyteller, and his personality was a big part of the draw. The other method of water bill payment was to hand Brother Tom a check on Sunday at Graisseville Baptist Church. A strange payment method if you didn't know that Brother Tom, our pastor, maintained our water system equipment. The mailbox was my payment method, mainly because I didn't read the paper and I didn't want to bother Brother Tom on Sundays.

As I drove to town to pay my water bill, I headed to the coffee shop for a large newly legalized café americano. The shop was two doors down from the *Gazette*, so I couldn't help but notice a crowd of agitated people standing outside the doors. Why not get involved?

"What's going on?" My question was met with a sea of angry faces. Maybe not a sea exactly, maybe more like a small creek.

"That dadgum Hugh closed the *Gazette* for a so-called family emergency. What are we going to do?"

The crowd became ugly, showing signs of a potential mob—at least in my mind. Deputy Chris Landry (Maggie's cousin) arrived on the scene in his parish-issued vehicle. He lived in Graisseville, which was also his primary patrol area. Chris was in a unique situation that qualified him for a parish-sponsored program using alternative patrol vehicles. The deputy had put in a request for a motorcycle, thinking that type of vehicle would be popular with the ladies and command respect as an officer of the law. But the government has a logic few can understand, and the state issued him a different type of transportation. Chris received a patrol transport that was more energy efficient, less expensive to maintain, and had greater maneuverability. It was a dream to park in the tiny downtown parking spaces. The car was also bright yellow, similar to a banana. Chris' ride was a smart car.

Graisseville Tires 'n' More, which serviced all the patrol cars, did not have a light bar that fit the newest member of the fleet. There was no money in the budget to purchase a customized light bar, so the mechanics improvised. They took a light bar off a decommissioned sedan and put it on Chris' ride. The light bar was too long to fit across the car. The geniuses placed it down the middle of the roof from the front to the back. That solution meant that no one in front or back of Chris could see the flashing red and blue lights. Our quick-thinking deputy spotted a set of battery-operated blinking Christmas lights on clearance and had an idea. He bought them and wrapped them around the top of his car's windshield, through the open windows, and back again, round and round. During the few times, Chris needed his lights, he would turn on the LED switch, and the Christmas lights would blink red and green. The other deputies took pity on Chris and hosted enough fundraisers to purchase a customized light bar. They promised to raise enough money to paint his ride a respectable forest green, like the other patrol cars. Should I state the obvious? Chris was still single.

"Hold up, ladies and gents, what seems to be the problem?"

Chris did a great job as our parish-issued deputy, and the other residents felt the same. They certainly treated Chris with a great deal of respect and admiration.

"Now listen here, Landry! Hugh closed the office, and we can't pay our water bills!"

Okay, not always respectful and not always full of admiration. Chris was not concerned.

"Calm down, Moe, you can still pay your bill in front of the water tank."

Even I knew that was not the issue. Those people weren't going to get the scoop on the upcoming paper. Wanting to help out, I intervened.

"Deputy Landry, these good people are more interested in what's going to be in the paper. By paying their bills at the water tank, they will miss out on the scoop from Hugh." Next, I addressed the mob, who were fast becoming my tribe. "What if we called Hugh and put him on speakerphone? He could tell us what's going to be in the paper."

My tribe nodded in agreement, and Chris breathed a sigh of relief.

"Hey, Jen, that's great, but could we do it somewhere else? Say Maggie's coffee shop? Ruby won't like a crowd standing outside, blocking the sidewalks of downtown."

Scanning both sides of the sidewalk, I saw no traffic— pedestrian, or otherwise. But I could definitely respect Chris wanting to remain on Ruby's good side.

"Yes! Let's all head to the coffee shop."

Everyone ordered a coffee drink, many ordered pastries, and Maggie and I figured out how to put Hugh on the big-screen TV. As everyone munched on their treats, Hugh regaled us with stories coming up in the paper. He shared stories not factual enough to print but still made good conversation. He also included his family emergency story. Hugh's granddaughter had the measles, and she needed a caregiver while her parents went to work. Hugh made it sound much more exciting, which was why people loved to chat with him.

Chris took me aside. "Jen, you saved the day! I really appreciated your help. You take care and I'll see you later."

My favorite deputy got into his smart car and the rest of us stayed a while longer to enjoy the company. I offered to take everyone's payments to the water tank mailbox and earned some more points with the town.

A few days later, Hugh called Maggie. "Could you do me a big favor and host all the weekly scoop meetings? That would free up a lot of my time, and office space. If you could teach me how to record my show, so to speak, I think we could do this."

The coffee shop hosted a weekly "Hanging with Hugh" segment, Maggie's sales increased, Hugh had his newspaper office back, and people started using the water tank mailbox. Of course, I took full credit and declared myself one of the people. My husband and Maggie were strangely silent, knowing pride goes before a fall.

CHAPTER 12—A FUNERAL FOR LEROY

Two weeks before Thanksgiving, which didn't mean much weather-wise in the South. The leaves don't change into a beautiful golden orange and drift slowly down to the earth. Instead, they turn brown and fall unceremoniously on the ground. The weather doesn't become crisp and smells like smoke from burning fireplaces. It maintains a balmy sixty degrees or so, give or take.

We Southerners spend our fall and winter in layers to prepare for the quick temperature changes. We begin the morning bundled up in a hoodie or jacket enjoying the forty- or fifty-degree weather, then shed our long sleeves around 10:00 a.m. for the remaining daylight hours. As the sun goes down, if we are still outside, we retrieve our outer layer of clothing until we return indoors. We may not have many seasons down here, but we also don't shovel snow or put chains on our vehicles. It's more than a fair trade.

While picking up the boys from Darla's daycare, I heard the news of Leroy's death. With tears in her eyes, Darla met me at the door. "Oh, Miss Jen! Have you heard the news? Leroy just passed away this afternoon. Oh, it's awful—just awful!"

Who the heck was Leroy? "Oh, I hadn't heard, Darla. But you're right—that is just awful. Do you know the plans for the funeral?"

Darla wiped a tear. "Oh, I'm sure they'll have a beautiful memorial service, but I can't imagine it would be an open casket. I expect the service will be in a few days. I'll be sure and let you know as soon as I hear."

As I said my goodbyes and took the boys to the car, I hoped a call to Maggie would solve the mystery. Her coffee shop closed at 5:00 p.m., so I called her on the way home. She didn't answer. My curiosity was burning a hole in my heart, second only to the irritation that I couldn't ask questions without sounding like I didn't know anything. I had lived in Graisseville for about five months, and I was tired of being the new girl. I tried to not ask questions except to Maggie and Mike. And my mother-in-law, of course.

Ava! My mother-in-law would have the scoop, and all it required was a quick detour.

She met me at the door with flour on her face and a small plate of cookies for sampling. The boys grabbed cookies and ran into the living room to see Pops.

"Jenny, you've got to try these pillowcase cookies."

What the heck were pillowcase cookies? Definitely the time to try one. Mmmm...they tasted like sugar cookies, but denser like a biscuit. These treats are unique to Cajun cuisine. Before heading back to the oyster reef in Lafourche Parish, oystermen would pack pillowcases full of these delights. The cookies survived the cold and moisture on the reefs, so their texture is a cross between a sugar cookie and hard tack. Never tasting hard tack for obvious reasons, I will gladly testify to the taste and quality of those cookies. I wouldn't turn down a pillowcase full of them if I was headed out to the oyster reefs.

My hands circled around my mother-in-law in a quick hug. "Ava, did you hear that Leroy passed away?"

I had to be quick with Ava because she would spend a lot of time giving me information. It was my job to sort through it, choosing what was helpful and what was not.

"Oh, yes, I did. Isn't that so sad? Leroy was a pillar of this community! We all loved him, and I just can't imagine what we will do without him."

Not helpful, not helpful at all. Why won't you give me Leroy's life story like you do with every other person? "Oh, Ava, I know. It really is just so sad. How is his family handling his death?" This had to be an opening Ava couldn't resist.

My mother-in-law frowned, her eyebrows pushed down deep in thought. "Why, Jen, I don't think Leroy had any family. You know, that really is sad. But he had so many friends that I'm sure he didn't mind. He was adored by the community, especially the children. I know for certain that at every football and basketball game, the kids would gather around him and practically hug him to death. I can't bear to think of those poor children going to the next sporting event and not getting to hug on sweet Leroy." She teared up and turned away to wipe her eyes.

Not much to go on, but it would have to do. My Crock-Pot of chili needed stirring, so I gave Walt a hug and grabbed the boys. "Jenny, you must take some pillowcase cookies home. I'm making them for Leroy's funeral."

"But you don't even know when it is!"

Ava headed back to the kitchen. "It's always a good idea to have baked goods on hand, in case of emergencies. Here are two dozen, for Mike and the boys."

I handed the container of cookies to Henry, picked up James, and we headed out to the Jeep.

Mike had been getting home at a reasonable hour every evening, thanks to Jimmy Melancon and his mom Amy. Mike had employed Amy to do the bookkeeping and payroll for his two employees. She also watched the store while Mike left early to pick up the boys for ice cream at the Dairy Delight. He was finally enjoying being a business owner, and that made him the man I fell in love with several years ago.

As we said the blessing over supper and I spooned out the chili (mac and cheese for James, our picky eater), I put my plan into motion.

"Did you hear about Leroy passing away? Isn't that just so sad?" Would Mike know anything about this mysterious Leroy?

Mike's eyes never stirred from his bowl of chili. "Yes, it is sad. Pass the cornbread please."

Huh? For a small town that shares information like peanut brittle, these townsfolk were letting me down. Even my own husband.

"Well, when I picked up the kids, Darla told me that she'd let me know about the funeral. I assume you'd like to go, right?"

Mike's eyes narrowed. "Uh, sure. Yeah, I think that would be the right thing to do. Be sure and let me know when you hear any news."

Mike wasn't one to gossip, so I wasn't surprised he didn't know any details about poor Leroy's passing. As his helpful wife, I'd offer all the details I had.

"I stopped by to see your mom, and she mentioned he was beloved by the community, especially the children." I was also hoping Mike would add to my small pool of knowledge.

"Oh, how are Mom and Dad? I really need to get by and see them." Changing the subject? Mike knew something but wasn't telling me.

"Okay, spill. You know something about Leroy." I gave him one of my *mom* looks, but Mike didn't flinch.

He returned my gaze, not even blinking. "Actually, Jen, I really don't know anything about Leroy. He came to town after I'd left for college. But I know he was a respected member of the community, and he will be missed. I really would like to go to the funeral. Do you know if my dark-blue suit is clean?"

Well, of course, Mike didn't have much information. He'd left Graisseville right after high school graduation about ten years ago and rarely returned. My husband would not be any more help.

Mike took the boys upstairs for baths and bedtime. I began to clean up the kitchen and dining room. As I was clearing the table, my mind processed the bits of information I'd collected during the day. Leroy had lived in the village no more than ten years. He had no family but lots of friends. Why would he have moved here if not for family? I decided to call Maggie to gather more information. I was on a mission and needed more intel.

"Hey, Jen, could I call you back? We're in the middle of bedtime." I would not be thwarted. I needed information.

"Sorry, Maggie, but I only need you for a minute. I heard Leroy passed away. Mike didn't know Leroy because he'd already moved away before Leroy moved here. Ava said Leroy didn't have any family but had lots of friends here in the community, so I was wondering why Leroy moved to Graisseville." I waited in anticipation of the missing pieces to my puzzle.

"Umm, well, I know the high school principal brought him to Graisseville. So I guess he moved here for his job? I think he used to be with Bob Cahill, on Bob's farm. But farming is hard work, and Leroy got too old for it. He wasn't quite ready to retire completely, I guess, so the principal told Bob he was happy to have Leroy come to the high school."

My excitement grew as I fit the new pieces into place. Leroy was a hard worker and hadn't been ready to retire. How kind and generous of that principal! Few people would find a place for a man older in years like Leroy. Tears spilled down my cheeks. If only I could hug that principal!

"Thanks, Maggie, I really appreciate your time. Give the girls hugs for me!" My sleuthing had been a success!

My next task was to head upstairs to kiss the boys good night and help them say prayers. "Boys, let's pray that Leroy is sitting in heaven right now, rejoicing before God. And let's pray that God would comfort Leroy's family wherever they are. Amen!"

Did Mike stifle a laugh? No, just a coughing fit. A really long coughing fit.

When I picked up the boys the next day, Darla grabbed my arm. "Oh, Miss Jen! The funeral for Leroy is Saturday at 10:00 a.m. in the high school gym."

What a fitting venue, since Leroy gave the last years of his life helping at the school! No wonder the kids all loved him so much and overwhelmed him with hugs.

My friend Google gave me the closest flower shop, Gidley Flowers in Zachary. I ordered the nicest funeral spray seventy-five dollars could buy. Although Mike had never met Leroy, I wanted to splurge and show my appreciation for the dearest man I would never meet. I also made sure Mike's dark-blue suit and white dress shirt were hanging in the closet, ready for Saturday.

When Mike came home from work, I told him about the funeral and asked if he'd be able to attend.

"Oh, I wouldn't miss this for the world, Jen! I've already asked Amy and Jimmy to watch the store Saturday morning."

My eyes swam with tears as I was reminded of how dear a man I'd married. Ava was attending the service, but Walt offered to stay home and watch the kids. " I told Mom we'd swing by and pick her up for the service."

As everything fell into place, I said a small prayer of thanks for Leroy and his service to Graisseville.

I called Ava on Friday, to ask if I should bring any food.

"Don't worry about it, dear, I've made enough pillowcase cookies for the entire community. But you did order flowers, right? From the flower shop?"

"Oh yes! Gidley's Flower Shop promised to send a beautiful arrangement of flowers over to the funeral home today." I literally heard disapproval over the phone lines.

"Oh no, dear, that's the wrong flower shop. You should have used Mason's, on Central Street in Zachary. We don't use Gidley's."

Seriously? How did one use the wrong flower shop?

"You'll have to call Gidley's and cancel the order."

I just had to ask. "I don't understand, Ava. Why can't we use Gidley's?"

Ava didn't miss a beat. "Because we've always used Mason's on Central Street. I've got to go. My timer just went off. Pick me up at 9:00 a.m. tomorrow because it's going to be crowded."

My glance confirmed the time as 3:00 p.m. I wasn't going to try to cancel the order that late in the day. What were the odds Ava was going to find out? The odds were ever in my favor.

We arrived at Walt and Ava's at 9:10 a.m., a minor miracle. The boys were still in their pajamas, and I hadn't brought clothes for them. Babysitting with Pops consisted of frozen waffles and Saturday morning cartoons while Pops read the paper and dozed. He would not get them dressed, so I wasn't going to waste my time. Mike and I, however, cleaned up pretty well in our dress clothes, and that helped offset our children.

I brought the boys to the door just as Ava opened it. She had her hands full with a tray of cookies and managed to stay balanced as her energetic grandsons blew past her into the living room.

"Pops, you're awesome!" Yeah, Walt just handed out some sort of food I didn't allow at home. Grandparents have earned the right to spoil their grandchildren, and I was okay with that.

Ava handed her tray to Mike and we all piled into my Wrangler. We were off to the funeral.

"Jenny dear, did you call and get your flowers changed to the right flower shop?"

Dang it, Ava! How could this woman remember these things? I went with the semi-honest answer. "I called Gidley's, and it was too late. But I will certainly remember for the future and only order flowers from Mason's on Central Street in Zachary."

Yeah, I was going to hear about my mistake at least until we arrived at the high school gym parking lot. Ava started with stories of people who'd ordered from Gidley's and regretted their decision to their dying days. She continued with the entire lineage on both her and Walt's sides of the family who had frequented Mason's and were blessed by God for their obedience. The woman concluded by detailing a list of flower orders she had placed over the last ten years and rated each one on a scale of one to ten. Not surprisingly, they all rated eight stars and above. I had never been so thankful to arrive at a funeral in my relatively short lifetime.

Ava wasn't wrong—the entire village had turned out for Leroy's funeral. I teared up again and thanked God for this amazing man who had given so much to our community. We walked in the door, and an usher handed me a program. I glanced at the front and saw an image of the high school mascot, the Fighting Mules.

That is just so fitting! My heart overflowed with warmth.

An usher led us to the middle of the bleachers, and I felt grateful we had received these wonderful seats. I was so glad I had come. Mike returned from delivering Ava's tray of pillowcase cookies for the reception. As he sat beside me, I grabbed his hand and squeezed it gently. He looked over with a quizzical look, and I smiled warmly. I hoped we would be as beloved in this community one day as dear Leroy was.

The principal stepped to the podium and asked everyone to take a seat. "Thank you. Please remain for the reception following the service, at the back of the gym. Let us bow our heads. Gracious Heavenly Father, we come here today to give tribute to a dear friend, Leroy. He blessed us with many years of loyal service, and we all know he is in a better place. Amen."

After the prayer, the principal clicked the button for the slideshow. The image of a mule stared back at me from the large screen, the same image that was on the front of my program. Maybe the slides were out of order? The slides were not out of order.

As various images of mules flashed on the screen, the principal's voice boomed across the gym. "Farmer Bob Cahill purchased Leroy from Merle's Auction Barn, on a beautiful spring day about seventeen years ago. Our friend worked faithfully on the Cahill farm carrying supplies for Bob as he rode his horse along the fence lines. After almost a decade of service, Leroy became too old to carry those heavy loads. Five years ago Farmer Bob approached me, asking if the school could adopt Leroy as their mascot. Being the Fighting Mules, I was delighted to agree. The school board approved a budget allocation for Leroy's feeding and veterinary needs, and the shop class built a pen for Leroy. Until this past week, Leroy was our mascot at all our high school sporting events. He has been a pillar of the community, adored by all. He especially loved children and welcomed hugs and pets from everyone."

I dropped Mike's hand faster than a hot pan of biscuits, my stare boring through him like a laser beam. My husband couldn't even look me in the eye, what with his body shaking with laughter. My eyes teared up with anger and humiliation. How could my husband allow me to believe Leroy was a human being? My stomach twisted, forming knots hard as rocks. I'd spent seventy-five dollars on a funeral arrangement for a mule! My emotions fluctuated from angry to humiliated, then back to angry. I'd have to play the pantry game for the next few weeks, pulling cans and bags out of the pantry to prepare meals. All because I'd blown my grocery budget on flowers for a mule. And back to being angry again!

Mike, Mike who? I refused to acknowledge my husband at the reception. Why didn't I bring a bigger purse? With all the food, I could have stashed our dinner for the next few weeks.

"Dear, would you like to take some leftovers home?" Before I could answer, someone handed me four foam containers. A virtual stranger knew how many family members I had, and I was grateful. I stuffed those containers with all food resembling meat and shoved the finished product into Mike's hands.

Ava stood by her friends, a circle of ladies crying quietly in the corner. Time to gather my family and head home.

"Oh, Jen, wasn't that just the most wonderful service you have ever attended? I never met Leroy personally, but I feel as if I had." She wiped her tears away and patted my hand. "Are you ready to go?"

At least Ava didn't realize my mistake. I studied the ladies' faces and realized something interesting. These women knew Leroy was only a mule, yet they grieved for him as if he was a human being. But why?

After we'd settled into the Jeep, I questioned Ava. "I'm curious. If you knew Leroy was a mule, why were you treating his death as if he was a human being?"

She blinked twice. "Why dear, he was still a part of our community! Human or animal, people loved him. He brought a lot of joy into our lives. The school events won't be the same without him, and I'm sure the children will miss him for a very long time."

My knots melted like butter in a skillet as I processed her words. Mike, sensing my mood, offered his sage advice.

"Small towns celebrate and honor our hometown heroes. Even though Leroy was a mule, he was a celebrity of sorts. I remember feeling ashamed in high school because I was a Fighting Mule. I always thought it sounded lame, and I remember my friends feeling the same way. I've noticed though since we've moved back, kids here have more pride in the school and the mascot. Leroy personified the Fighting Mules and put a face to a name, so to speak. We were one of just a few local schools that had an actual mascot, not just some guy dressed up in an outfit more suited for the dumpster. I, for one am sad Leroy has passed. And I hope after the appropriate time of mourning the school will get another live mascot." He glanced at me in the rearview mirror and smiled.

I wasn't ready to forgive him, but I acknowledged his points. My anger had finally left the building, but humiliation and a sense of destitution still occupied my heart.

We stepped into Ava's house, Mike following with the empty plate. The boys grabbed my legs and rubbed their sticky faces on my dress. Dang it! I'd hoped to hang the dress straight up in the closet and avoid a cleaning bill, but that would not be the case.

Walt woke up when the boys squealed at our entrance. "Oh, how ya'll doing? We've had a great time while you've been gone." A great time napping while the boys ran the roads, no doubt. "How was the funeral?"

"Oh, honey, it was a fine affair! Well, except for the few arrangements from Gidley's Flower Shop. But the ones from Mason's were quite beautiful."

A perfect opportunity to make our exit. "Goodbye! See you tomorrow at church."

Mike took my hand as we exited Walt and Ava's driveway. "Babe, I know you're mad at me, and I'm sorry. I wasn't making fun of you, I really wasn't. I love how you embraced Leroy's passing so enthusiastically, even if you thought he was a man. I am so proud of how you've adopted Graisseville and all its eccentricities, and you are taking the time to become part of the community. I should have told you straight up that Leroy was a mule, and I am sorry I didn't. Am I forgiven?"

Oh, this man was just too cute—how could I stay mad? "Well, I'm glad you see my efforts. I'm really trying to fit into this community, and it's nice that you appreciate them."

Mike parked the Jeep a forgiven man. We entered our completely renovated barn home, stopping in the kitchen to deposit the foam containers.

Mike wrapped me in a big bear hug. "Tell me, what did you think of Leroy's service?"

My brain reflected on the morning's events. "It was beautiful, and there was so much love in that school gymnasium. Of course, the food was amazing, as always. All the flowers were beautiful. Oh, and I found the funeral arrangement we sent. It turned out very nice, well worth the money."

Mike kissed me on the forehead. "Oh good! But you know...it would have been nicer if you'd gotten it from Mason's. On Central Street in Zachary." His hands grabbed my shoulders and pushed me back a couple of steps, giving him room to turn and bolt for the closest exit.

To this day, there is a dent just to the right of the entrance to our living room from the kitchen, where a cast-iron skillet hit the wall.

CHAPTER 13—THE DECEPTIVE PLAYDATE

The move from our one-room farm home into our renovated barn went relatively smoothly. There were no catastrophes or incidents worth mentioning. Even the renovation process was smooth, and we had Maggie's brother, Charlie, to thank. Mike's best friend from high school was our general contractor, and he took care of us. He was also my best friend's brother, which didn't hurt a bit.

We purchased our property in April, moved in May, and moved into our barn home in September. I hosted Thanksgiving and invited my parents to join us. My sister and her family had other plans, and we missed them. Mike's brother Joe was working the holiday, in his big city law firm in Shreveport.

My mother and mother-in-law were as different as night and day, but they agreed with two statements of opinion. "Jen and Mike are just perfect for each other! And they produced the two most perfect human beings on the planet!"

All other opinions never made it in the door. My father and father-in-law spent Thanksgiving in front of the television, arguing over college football. Our holiday was stress-free, which landed me in December feeling on top of the world.

I volunteered in the church nursery one Sunday a month, getting to know the tinier members of my church. I also got to know the moms and dads as they picked up their children, which was how I met Annelise.

Annelise Trahan had a child in the nursery and was the special events coordinator for our church. She was bubbly and cheerful, a little too much so for me personally, but I liked her well enough. She coordinated our Trunk or Treat event in October, and the Christmas program. Being new in town, I was a blank slate for Annelise and her efforts.

"Jen, hi! How are you? How did my Jep do today?"

Annelise's son, born two weeks before James, had quickly become his best church friend. The toddler friendship made me consider a playdate, but I hadn't pulled the trigger. Could I handle that much bubbliness and cheerfulness at one time?

"Hey, Annelise! Jep did great today! He and James played the entire time and never squabbled." As I handed her Jep's bag, I affirmed my decision. Definitely not time to invite them over. When I heard her voice, my brain conjured the fountain in New Orleans' Audubon Park.

But Annelise hadn't sensed my hesitation. "Oh, Jen! I'd love to have you and James over this afternoon for a playdate. After nap time of course. Would you be available?"

Oh, okay, so this was happening. Mike said I needed to branch out and have more friends. He was probably right, but who could be a better friend than my coffee dealer? James and Jep got along well in the nursery, so it made sense to try a playdate. But did three-year-old boys really need a social circle?

"Let me check with Mike and make sure he's okay with watching Henry. But I suppose so."

"Great! I'll see you at four. In case you don't know, I live on Holly Street, in the two-story with the blue shutters. We're across from Al and Ruby Bergeron. This is going to be so much fun!"

No one gave out addresses in small towns, just the street name and their neighbor. If you were lucky, they'd throw in a short description of the house. I got lucky.

"Now, don't you bring anything! I'll have some coffee and a snack for us, and something fun for the boys."

Nope, I wouldn't fall for that either. Hostesses insisted a guest bring nothing but were annoyed if the guest actually brought nothing. That part I already knew from growing up in a standard small Southern town.

After putting the boys down for naps and getting Mike's buy-in, I surveyed my pantry for inspiration. I was coming off my pantry purge from dropping seventy-five dollars on Leroy's funeral arrangement. I hadn't gotten paid yet, so I was going to use what I had. Or was I?

"Hey, Ava! How are you? Good. Yes, Brother Tom's sermon was inspiring. Speaking of inspiring, Annelise Trahan invited James and me to her house this afternoon. Yes, that is exciting! My pantry isn't inspiring me, and I wondered if you have any ideas for some easy cookies or a cake." No doubt Ava had something in the oven she could share.

"Oh, honey, you don't need to go to the trouble of baking something. I have a Louisiana crunch cake in the oven I'm happy to give you. I was just making it for Walt and me to eat this week. But I can make another."

Bless that woman's heart as she saved me once again! Ava also knew where Annelise lived, so that was a bonus. "Her exact address is 502 Holly Street. You can put that in your phone and find it in a jiffy!"

Louisiana crunch cake is a Bundt cake also known as a Sock-It-to-Me cake. It has pecans and cinnamon and will make a person cry tears of joy while devouring it. My father actually shed tears while consuming several pieces at Thanksgiving.

Many recipes call for a yellow cake mix, but Ava Guidry would not allow any type of prepackaged food into her kitchen. This cake was the perfect gift to bring to my playdate with a founding family member. I drove to Ava's, retrieved the cake, and verbalized my unwavering loyalty to her baking genius.

Promptly at 3:48 p.m., James and I were on the road, destination 502 Holly Street. This was a good idea, and I did need to make more friends. Maybe Annelise would become as dear to me as Maggie.

We arrived just six minutes late, thanks to Annelise living eighteen minutes from our house. Most likely I'd never be on time for any playdate, at least until the kids were old enough to get ready without parental intervention.

Annelise and Jep greeted us at the door. Mmmm, was that a hint of approval as she inspected the cake? The boys ran to Jep's bedroom, and we taller humans settled into the living room. Annelise had laid out coffee cups, dessert plates, and what looked to be a small binder. My curiosity was aroused.

"Jen, I'm so glad you agreed to meet me this afternoon. I really do appreciate it."

Annelise poured the coffee and served the Louisiana crunch cake, What was that weird vibe? This was a social visit, wasn't it?

"Jen, your efforts in our community have not gone unnoticed. Our church leaders are impressed with the time you're spending in the nursery. We would like to offer you a promotion."

Uh-oh! This woman was going to ask me to be in charge of something, wasn't she?

"Graisseville Baptist Church has a distinguished history of hosting our community's Living Nativity on the day before Christmas Eve, the twenty-third of December. Our past nativity coordinator, Anna Dunbar, is getting along in years and needs to pass the baton, so to speak. The church leaders have prayed diligently and asked God to show us who should oversee the Living Nativity. God answered our prayers, Jen! He told us He wants you to coordinate this year's event. What do you think?"

Annelise leaned back on the couch and took a sip of coffee. She hadn't touched her cake. She didn't look like she'd ever given birth either. Coincidence? I think not. Suddenly, I didn't feel much like eating either.

"Annelise, I appreciate your faith in me. Could I have some time to pray about it, and talk to my husband?"

Her smile didn't waver, but her eyes darkened. "I certainly understand, Jen, and I respect your response. But you should ask God to give you an answer quickly. We have less than a month to get this show on the road."

Things got a little awkward. I didn't want to scoop up James and flee, but I'd been deceived. Why not flip through the binder? As I glanced at the pages, I saw detailed notes from past Living Nativities. Anna Dunbar had documented a detailed plan of execution. Why, Jen—you could follow her step-by-step project plan and pull off this special event with little effort. My wheels were turning.

"Annelise, I've made my decision. If God wants me to coordinate the reenactment of the birth of His only Son, then who am I to disagree? I am honored to take on this project."

A whoosh of air from Annelise's lungs—a sure sign she'd had no backups in her pocket. The woman actually picked up her crunch cake! My eager hands reached for my plate, and the rest of our afternoon became just another playdate. Even the image of the fountain in Audubon Park faded.

As I backed out of Annelise's driveway, a thought zipped into my head. You made a friend—that's two! Three if I counted Amy. "Dear Lord, thank You for my new friendship with Annelise, and my new responsibility. Please help me execute this new task. Amen!"

God, as always, did not disappoint. Many people said it was the most unique Living Nativity scene they had ever experienced. God does work in mysterious ways, especially at Christmas.

CHAPTER 14—THE LIVELY NATIVITY

A nnelise and I became close during December, as she helped me negotiate the binder. Once I had agreed to coordinate our Living Nativity, Annelise put into motion a traditional Graisseville promotional campaign. She placed an ad with the *Gazette*, the same as the previous year. The Living Nativity would be on December 23. The event would run from six to seven o'clock, lots of time for everyone to attend. Annelise photocopied flyers at her office and handed them out to local businesses. She posted weekly reminders on social media. Louisiana temperatures in December were normally in the fifties and sixties, so the weather should be perfect for an outdoor event.

Walt and Ava were over the moon that I was in charge of the Living Nativity. Ava offered to coordinate the mountains of treats to pass out, including the hot chocolate. As I scanned Anna Dunbar's binder, I realized just how easy this event should be. Task Number One: contact Hugh Cormier at the *Gazette*. Annelise took care of that, so check.

Task Number Two: contact Ava Guidry to coordinate food and drinks for participants and guests. Hey, I was breezing through this list faster than my husband could fall asleep during a Saints game!

Number three on the task list: contact the prior year participants and sign them up. Anna's list included a donkey, an ox, a couple of sheep, and a goat. A family east of the village actually owned a camel for the wise men. Anna's list also included chickens, ducks, and bunny rabbits for a petting zoo. My heart beat faster as I envisioned pure joy on children's faces while they lovingly nuzzled bunnies and ducks. This was going to be the best Living Nativity ever! Why did that comment sound familiar?

Oh yes, the book! Barbara Robinson wrote a wonderful book, *The Best Christmas Pageant Ever*. The cover of the book has the word "Worst" crossed out and the word "Best" written above it. It's a wonderful story about a woman who gets roped into producing and directing the annual children's Christmas pageant at her church. Through a series of unfortunate events, she ends up with some pretty sketchy actors. The pageant transforms into a production that touches everyone's hearts and causes them to think more deeply about the birth of Christ. Thank goodness I wouldn't have hardships like the director in that book! My Christmas showcase was going to be a snap.

My event rolled along with no problems, thanks to Anna's binder. Everyone agreed to take part, all free of charge. Anna's binder suggested a recently born child for the Son of God, but I decided to use a doll from the church nursery. I didn't want to leave anything to chance.

The Monday before Christmas, I contacted all the actors for our pre-scheduled rehearsal on December 22. My assembly crew put together the stable on December 21. The stable assembly went smoothly and so did our rehearsal. The animals weren't there, but their handlers understood the cues.

At the end of rehearsal, the owner of the camel raised his hand. "You know, the temperatures tomorrow night are supposed to drop to thirty-five degrees. I'm not hauling my camel over here if it's that cold."

The owners of the donkey, ox, sheep, goat, chickens, ducks, and bunny rabbits followed his lead, boycotting the cold temperatures. The animals could handle near-freezing temperatures, but the owners were more delicate. Most didn't even attend our church, so why suffer through the cold? I sensed a mutiny on my hands.

I prevailed upon community spirit, the spirit of the season, and any other spirits I could conjure. My rousing speeches swung the chicken, duck, and bunny owner. She lived in town and her sister attended our church. My camel man was a definite no if the temperature dropped to thirty-five degrees or below, and he carried the donkey, ox, sheep, and goat votes. We left the rehearsal with a consensus to watch the weather and make a final decision by 5:00 p.m. the next day.

My heart sank. I couldn't have a Living Nativity with only birds and bunnies. According to "Away in a Manger", the cattle are lowing, and the baby awakes. It definitely made no mention of bunnies or chickens or ducks.

Cattle? Cattle! I raced to Big Ed's where Mike was still on duty. "Hey, hello! How are you? I need a list of your cattle customers. Now!"

Mike stepped back, his face radiating suspicion. "Jen, that's confidential information. You need to tell me why."

Husbands can be so frustrating sometimes! "Because I need some backup animals for my Living Nativity!"

Mike placed his hands on his hips, deep in thought. "You know, you should really start with people who attend our church. I think they'd be more likely to help you. I'd call Ken Melancon first. He has a small herd of cows. I think he might have a donkey too."

Hmmm...Mike could be incredibly helpful sometimes. "Here, I just sent you Ken's contact information. Good luck!"

I called Ken from my Jeep and explained the situation. "Sure, Jen, I'm happy to be your Plan B—I've been called worse. Yeah, I can give you two steer and my donkey. Oh, I've got a goat too. And my nephew is raising a sheep for 4H. I bet he'd let you borrow it if you want."

Plan B was shaping up nicely—a couple of cows, a donkey, and even a sheep on standby. I could live without the goat—there was no mention of a goat in the Book of Luke, anyway. This Living Nativity was back in business!

Promptly at 8:00 a.m. on December 23, my phone blew up. The actors were reading the weather report, and they didn't like what they saw. My Joseph was getting sick, so he didn't want to be out in thirty-five-degree weather. A shepherd texted. He and his fellow shepherd were going out of town on Christmas Eve and couldn't risk getting sick. No doubt my Mary, the wise men, and my innkeeper would be contacting me soon, and my hoofed actors would be bailing too.

What do I do when the world lets me down? Stop by the coffee shop for coffee and a chat with Maggie. Along with caffeine, this girl needed some support. On the way to the coffee shop, I called Ken Melancon to put Plan B into action.

"Jen, I am really sorry to do this to you, but my cows have pink eye. So does my donkey. And my nephew really doesn't want you to use his sheep. It could win best show at the state fair, which means money for college. He doesn't want to risk that. I just feel so bad after all you and Mike have done for Jimmy and us. If I have any ideas though, I'll let you know."

As I disconnected the call, I felt the sting of tears in my eyes.

Maggie saw my car pull up and started making my latest favorite beverage. As I relayed the morning's disaster to her, she mixed in the peppermint and handed me my Jack Frost latte.

"You know, Jen, I have an idea. The Wheelers, the other Wheelers who own the dairy farm, might have something you can borrow. They used to have some cardboard cutouts of cows. They put them up in their front pasture to advertise their dairy farm. I think there might have been a farmer? You should give Ben Wheeler a call. Here, I'll share his contact with you."

My latte and I sat down at the nearest table to call Ben. When I explained the situation, Ben was sympathetic but confused.

"Maggie's thinking of my neighbor, Fred Dwyer. Yeah, ol' Fred used to put those out in his field. As he's gotten older, he's stopped. He probably still has them, but I'm not sure that's really what you're looking for."

I could have kissed Ben Wheeler, and given the situation, Mike probably wouldn't have cared.

"I'm sure they will be fine, Ben. Thanks again!"

Oops, I didn't have Fred's number. But Mike probably did. One call and my husband shared Fred's number, which I dialed immediately. After sipping some more Jack Frost latte of course. Yes, Jen—you can make this work!

On the phone, Fred sounded in his mid-seventies and talked much more slowly than I had time for. "Listen, Fred—I'll be over in twenty minutes to look at the animal cutouts."

I knew where the Wheeler Dairy Farm was, and Ben said Fred was his neighbor. Almost knocking over the table in my excitement, I stopped to take a breath. In farmer speak, that could mean the homes were twelve miles apart.

Who had time to drive all over rural East Baton Rouge Parish? "Where's Fred Dwyer's farm? Hurry, woman—where is it?"

Maggie's eyes resembled my Aunt Louise's white china platters. "Uh, I can share the pin that his granddaughter sent me, but I don't think..." She trailed off as I sprinted out the door. As I backed up my Jeep, I heard the notification on my phone.

Maggie had been out to the Dwyer's farm to bring coffee and pastries for a family reunion. Fred's granddaughter had pinned her location at the farm, then shared it with Maggie for the coffee delivery. It should take me right to the farm.

10:00 a.m., nine hours before the event. Everyone had officially texted or left me a voicemail, so I only had a stable and a manger. I called the bird and bunny owner to cancel and heard relief spilling out of the phone. On to Plan C!

In the driveway, I spotted an older man, a middle-aged woman, and a girl in her mid-twenties. I jumped out of the Jeep, narrowly dodging the farm dog. As my feet hit the front porch, I stopped and caught my breath. It was only 10:30 a.m.—why was I running? Plenty of time.

Fred introduced me to his daughter, Janelle, and granddaughter, Faith. The three Dwyers led me to the barn where the animal cutouts were stored. Except they weren't animal cutouts, they were produce cutouts.

"I tried to tell you on the phone, Mrs. Guidry, but you'd already hung up. We aren't dairy farmers like the Wheelers. We grow broccoli, carrots, cauliflower, cucumbers, tomatoes, peppers, and corn."

Good to know. I gazed at the five-foot plywood cutouts of happy dancing produce. My heart sank, and my eyes stung. But all was not lost—the Dwyers had Plan D.

Fred's daughter Janelle spoke up first. "Mrs. Guidry, my daughter and I are excellent seamstresses, even if I do say so myself. We were talking, and, well, what if we sewed costumes for the cutouts? We inspected them, and they're all in great shape. The tallest cutouts could be the men. Joseph can be the corn, the carrots could be the shepherds, and the wise men can be the cucumbers. We can sew robes and head coverings for them fairly easily." Her words shut off my waterworks.

Faith continued. "We found a pattern my mother used to make my brother's shepherd costume many years ago. We can change it to fit these cutouts. Mary can be the tomato. As you can see, the look on the tomato's face is almost angelic."

Yes, this might work! A smile crept on my face, signaling the women to unveil the rest of their plans.

"Now these cauliflowers are already white, like sheep. We just tack some black ears on them, and they'll be done. Easy peasy! The bell pepper can be the ox. Again, we just tack on some ears and a tail, and we're good to go. The broccoli is the only thing left, so it will have to be a camel. We can give it ears and a tail and a rope tying it to the cucumbers— as if the wise men are leading it to the stable."

My lungs exhaled the first deep breath all morning. "Yes, let's do it! It's a little unconventional, but these actors won't whine about the cold."

"Now we don't have a donkey. But we own a Shetland pony, and she doesn't mind the cold at all. I think if we stick her in the back of the stable, behind the cutouts, then it will be fine. The only thing we're missing is a Baby Jesus and a manger." My smile took over my face as I bought into the plan.

"Ladies, this is wonderful! We have a manger in the stable, already set up in front of the church. Could we get some hay for the manger?" Janelle nodded.

"Great! So all we need is a Baby Jesus. I was going to use a baby doll from the church nursery, but that would look ridiculous among the produce. Baby Jesus also needs to be a fruit or vegetable. Quick! Name produce that grows to about twenty-two inches!"

James' length at birth, was twenty-two inches. Surely the Son of God wouldn't be any bigger. My produce farmers were deep in thought, and Faith spoke up.

"The Baby Jesus should be smaller than that because our cutouts aren't life-size either."

Hmmm, she was right. So what should we use to represent our Lord and Savior? What type of produce would be respectful and honoring? Was any of this derailed nativity respectful and honoring toward God? I was starting to have my doubts.

Like hot fudge running down ice cream, peace took over my heart. The verses from 2 Corinthians 9:11 (ESV) drifted into my brain. "You will be enriched in every way to be generous in every way, which through us will produce thanksgiving to God."

All day long people in the community reached out to help me in my time of need. Many of them, like the Melancons, hadn't been able to come through, but they made every effort. The Dwyer family didn't even attend our church, but their generosity in time and talent was unmatched. Lord, You're going to pull off this nativity event, aren't You? As off the rails as our event had become, it would still give thanks to God and glorify Him.

Another word entered my head, but it came out of the mouth of Fred's daughter.

"Eggplant! I have an eggplant in my crisper! I was going to make Christmas aubergine for Christmas Eve supper. I can sew some swaddling clothes and wrap the eggplant! It's a good nine inches long."

Our play was cast, and our seamstresses left the barn to dig through Grandma Dwyer's stash of fabric. I turned to Fred, my heart at peace and a smile as big as the Pontchartrain River. "Now, Fred, how can we get these actors to their set before 7:00 p.m. tonight?"

"My son-in-law and grandson will load everything on the trailer and bring them to the church. Don't you worry, Mrs. Guidry, we're not going to let you or God down." Of course, the Dwyer family had logistics covered. My arms circled around Mr. Dwyer's shoulders, scaring him a little.

My Jeep and I headed back to the coffee shop to give Maggie the good news. Just before I pulled onto the highway, I glanced down at my phone. Why had Annelise been calling and texting? Fifteen texts and seven missed calls in the last hour? And it was almost noon, confirmed by my stomach. As I dialed Annelise's number to share my good news, gurgles exploded from my stomach.

"Jen, where have you been? Never mind! I wanted to let you know I've canceled tonight's Living Nativity. After speaking with Brother Tom, we agreed it's just too cold."

No! This wasn't happening, not after all the work the Dwyers and I had put into Plan D. "Actually, Annelise, I've solved the problem, so I need you to uncancel tonight." I outlined my plan proudly, but Annelise was not impressed.

"Produce as the Holy Family? Certainly not! Tell the Dwyers they might as well stop making costumes. This plan is not happening."

No way was I going to let this woman have the final say. Why not go over her head? "What if I get Brother Tom to approve my changes? Then we can do this, right?"

"Oh, of course—absolutely! But that won't happen." She might be right—Brother Tom would never agree to an eggplant portraying the Lamb of God. But I had to try.

Where to begin? "Hello, Brother Tom—how are you today? Good, that's good. If you have a few minutes, I'd like to talk to you about the Living Nativity."

I began with the history of the event, how inspiring it was to the community, and that I didn't want to let down the village. Next, I outlined my initial problem—live humans canceling. I repeated my call to Ken Melancon for backup livestock and my trek to Fred Dwyer's farm, including the part where I thought the cutouts were cows and hopefully also people. Those details were important, so Brother Tom didn't think I jumped to cutouts of produce. I wanted him to know I was actually on Plan D. Did this confession make my plan seem better or worse? At that point, I wasn't certain.

Brother Tom stopped me after I described the Dwyer family's sewing talents. "Did you say Dwyer? Fred Dwyer, the produce farmer?"

"Yes, sir, I did."

Was that a rattle as Brother Tom shook his head? "You know, that man has not darkened the doorstep of a church in twenty years. I'm not sure what exactly happened. All I know is he's threatened to call the police on every person who's gone out there talking about church. That you convinced him to donate his time and talents to the Living Nativity is truly miraculous."

He paused, as if deep in thought. "On the surface, I would never agree to portray the Holy Family as fruits and vegetables. But God seems to be using you and this weather to reach Fred Dwyer and his family. I may not always understand our Father's ways, but I would never stand in defiance of those ways, either. I think you should go ahead with your Living Nativity event. Produce Nativity event? What is it exactly you're calling it now?"

A laugh escaped my mouth—that was the farthest thing from my mind. "Well, sir, I really have no idea. I was just so excited to get to this step in the journey."

Brother Tom chuckled as well. "I will pray for you, Jen, and your Lively Nativity. If there is anything I can do for you, please do not hesitate to let me know."

One thing jumped to the front of my mind. "Could you please call Annelise and tell her you've approved my 'Lively Nativity'? I'm not sure she'd believe me."

Another chuckle. "Of course! I'll deliver the good news to Annelise myself."

My call ended just as I pulled in front of the coffee shop. Thank goodness they were open! There was so much news to share with Maggie!

We improved the Lively Nativity by making it a drive-in event. Everyone could stay in their cars to keep warm and turn their radio stations to KLGT FM 101.7 (KAY-LIGHT). KLGT was the nearest faith-based radio station and played holiday songs through Christmas Day.

Maggie called the station, described our Lively Nativity, and asked the DJ to play faith-based Christmas music from 7:00 to 9:00 p.m. He promised to do his best and offered to mention us on the radio. What great news!

It was almost 2:00 p.m., and I still hadn't had lunch. Thank goodness the Gas 'n' More offered food. Maggie and I munched on pizza and discussed what we would be wearing for our drive-in Lively Nativity. We flooded social media, and I ran next door to the *Gazette*. "Could you advertise our event on the newspaper's social media sites?"

Maggie texted Mayor Ruby's grandson, who handled the village's social media, and asked him to start flooding the internet.

The Dwyers arrived at the church promptly at 6:00 p.m. with all the cutouts and costumes, including the eggplant. They also brought ham sandwiches, chips, and bottled water, so we could fuel up for the long night ahead. Mike left Amy and Jimmy to close Big Ed's, so he could help unload and set up. He brought the boys with him, and they marveled at the five-foot stalk of corn dressed as the earthly father of our Savior.

Ken Melancon arrived, wanting to pitch in. We had everything in place and ready to go by 6:45 p.m., just in time for Ava and her brigade to arrive with hot chocolate and baked goods. Cars were already lining up in the church parking lot. This Lively Nativity would exceed my expectations!

The Dwyers stuck around to hand out hot chocolate and treats. Maggie arrived with coffee, scarves, hats, and gloves. The night flew by as we sped back and forth between snacks and cars. The hot chocolate was long gone, along with the baked goods. It was 8:15 p.m. and way past Henry and James' bedtime. Ava sat in Walt's truck, holding a sleeping James.

"Hey, Ava—could you and Walt take the boys home for the night?"

As I watched the line of never-ending cars, I felt a sense of wonder. All those people were coming to see our Lively Nativity! Although I hadn't attended the year before, I knew we'd long surpassed previous numbers. My heart stayed warm, despite the freezing temperatures.

Where was Henry? Walt and Ava were ready to leave. There he was, standing beside the stable holding Mike's hand.

"I like the cauliflower sheep, Dad, I think they're my favorite. Which ones are your favorite?"

Could my heart be any fuller? What a wonderful male bonding moment.

"I like the broccoli, son, mostly because it looks nothing like a real camel."

Those two Guidry men had a short but deep discussion about the scene in front of them and what it represented to the world. My eyes teared up for at least the third or fourth time that day, but they were finally tears of joy. That moment made the stresses of the day worthwhile.

Henry paused a moment as he processed Mike's words, how God sent his Son to die for the world because His love for us knows no bounds.

"I think I understand pretty much what you're saying, Dad. But why did Mom choose an eggplant for Baby Jesus?"

My breathing stopped, wondering what profound thoughts my husband would put together. Perhaps Baby Jesus seemed so fragile like an eggplant seems fragile? But in reality, He was strong enough to save the world, just as an eggplant's exterior is strong and tough. I crept forward just enough to hear Mike's words of wisdom.

"Oh, that's easy, Henry. The eggplant was in the crisper."

CHAPTER 15—THE BACKUP BEAUTY QUEEN

Louisiana hosts more festivals than the calendar has days. We celebrate crawfish, meat pies, pirates, and boudin. We even recognize rougarous, the Cajun French version of a werewolf that lurks in the swamps.

Most of our festivals crown a queen during the celebration. These young ladies maintain high grade point averages, cultivate memberships in multiple respected societies and clubs, and dream of lofty aspirations beyond high school. According to the Pirate Festival website, there isn't a Queen of the Pirates. Hopefully, her time is coming. I, for one, would enjoy wearing my Queen of the Pirates crown as I pushed my cart among the produce at my local grocery store. Who wouldn't want to sport a sash and tiara while sorting through melons and tomatoes? It is a prestigious honor to be the home of a festival queen, and our small village took it seriously.

With high hopes, Graisseville had entered a contestant for the last decade, anticipating her success. Each time, the young lady returned with her head bare. Our village mantra became *next year*. In the eleventh year, we actually believed it. That year would be our triumph. That was the year of Aurelie Hebert.

Aurelie was enchanting. Her platinum-blonde hair trailed down her back in gentle waves, framing her turquoise eyes in wispy ringlets. Those eyes guaranteed our future queen never tied a shoe or carried a book as long as a teenage boy hung around. And they definitely hung around, circling Aurelie like sheep to Bo Peep.

The high school choir director compared her voice to Judy Garland. Our village gossip insisted that Carnival Cruise Lines approached Aurelie to sing on their cruises out of New Orleans. After graduation, of course.

Aurelie maintained a GPA of 4.1 while captain of the cheerleading squad and president of the National Honor Society. During the Miss Graisseville competition, she performed Whitney Houston's "I Will Always Love You" while twirling flaming batons. Several witnesses reported tears in the judges' eyes as she captured their hearts and their votes. No other Miss Graisseville scored so high in the contest's history. Aurelie seemed destined to win the festival crown. She took her destiny seriously.

Aurelie practiced day and night for the festival, according to the neighbors. They had Whitney's song burned into their brains and heard the tune in their sleep. They didn't mind because it was all in the name of community spirit. Aurelie's crown could put Graisseville on the map, so to speak. The win could pave the way for more tourism, leading to growth. Village growth would translate into new businesses, which meant more jobs and, therefore, more revenue. Aurelie had the potential to transform Graisseville into a larger, more affluent community.

Six weeks before the festival, Ava burst through the door of Maggie's shop. "Oh, it's awful, just awful! Aurelie Hebert has suffered a tragic baton accident and cannot compete at the festival. I can't believe it! What are we going to do?"

Wiping up the drops of my favorite brew as best I could, I glanced at my mother-in-law. A baton accident? How does that even happen? My best friend in high school wanted to try out for the majorette squad, so she bought a baton and began twirling. That girl practiced for hours but kept hitting herself on the head when she threw her baton in the air.

Her father finally threw the baton in the trash can. "I officially declare your twirling career finished! Our health insurance doesn't cover baton twirling injuries." Later, we discovered that wasn't true. Truthfully, though, her dad saved my friend from potential brain damage. From what I'd heard, Aurelie was much more coordinated.

Ava's voice returned me from memory lane as she wrung her hands, describing the tragedy. "Oh, it's horrible, just horrible! Aurelie was practicing with her flaming batons and singing her signature song. You know, that beautiful song by Whitney Houston! Well, the wind picked up, and a gust blew sparks off the batons into Aurelie's hair. Now, fortunately, Aurelie's father made her promise to always have a bucket of water and a hose nearby, just in case the batons caught fire to something. That quick-thinking gal ran over to the bucket and dunked her head to save the day."

My mind pictured all that long platinum hair as fuel for a fire. Thank goodness Mr. Hebert thought ahead!

"Our sweet Aurelie's quick thinking would have saved the day, except for her brother Elliott. That young man doesn't have the sense that God gave him! Why, when he was a little boy..."

Ava had a habit of going down rabbit trails before finishing her stories. I'd learned through the years that she just needed a nudge back to the main path. "Ava! What did Aurelie's brother do?"

My mother-in-law paused, frowned slightly, then found her footing. "Oh yes! Well, Aurelie's brother was supposed to water the flowers when he got home from school. His mama had been fussing at him to get it done all afternoon. Finally, his mama yelled, 'Elliott, if you don't water those flowers, I'm going to unplug that Xbox and throw it out the window!' So, Elliott got up off the couch, went outside, and poured the water into the flower bed."

By that time, all of us in the coffee shop tuned in to Ava's story. We also understood why Ava's voice had rose an octave, and her speech accelerated.

"That darn boy used Aurelie's bucket to water the flowers! And he didn't have the sense to refill it! So the poor girl didn't douse her curls with water—she just whacked her head on the bottom of the empty bucket! But Aurelie—oh, that girl's as smart as a whip! I'll give her credit for that! She ran to the faucet and turned on the hose."

Ava stopped for a breath, and we all took one with her. We'd not had this much excitement since Bob Cahill's cows got out on Highway 171, and the sheriff's deputies helped him push them off the road.

"By the time Aurelie put out her hair, most of it was gone. She ran in to get her mama, and they called Dr. Phillips. He recommended a hair and scalp specialist in Baton Rouge, and Mrs. Hebert called him next. But he said there was nothing he could do in the six weeks before the festival." Ava continued wringing her hands, as if she was wringing out a wet towel.

Our visions of a festival crown circled the drain. The Board of Aldermen called an emergency village council meeting to find a new Miss Graisseville. Ava sent her husband, so she could bake pecan sandies for Aurelie and her family. Wild horses couldn't keep me away from this meeting! How could we fix this disaster?

Mayor Ruby Bergeron spent the first fifteen minutes reviewing the facts of the situation. Aurelie had been our greatest hope, and now she could not fulfill her destiny. Three other young ladies had competed with Aurelie in the original Miss Graisseville competition. One of them fractured her wrist helping her father on the farm, and the second had gone to live with her aunt in New Orleans. The third potential Miss Graisseville temporarily resided in the parish detention center, awaiting trial for shoplifting at the Gas n' More. She would be out on bail by the festival, but no one wanted to put that on her application. Our prospects did not look promising.

Alderman Clay Terry called for order amid the murmurs of frustration and despair.

"Ladies and gentlemen, I may have a solution. My niece, Rose Terry, has a GPA just as high as Aurelie's. She is extremely talented and blessed with her grandmother's natural Bergeron family beauty. How about we select a committee to review her qualifications and reconvene in a couple of days?" Clay looked around the room, hoping we would embrace his plan.

"That's a wonderful idea, Clay! I mean, Alderman Clay. I mean, Alderman Terry." This speech sounded better in my head. "I volunteer to be on the review committee." Not to be left out of an adventure, Maggie quickly jumped in. Looking around the room, I saw a handful of people meeting my gaze. Amy took pity on me and raised her hand to be the third member of our merry band.

"Wonderful! Ava, could you nominate these fine ladies so we can vote to accept the committee? Then I suggest we meet back here in three days and hear the committee's recommendation. Do I hear a second?" Clay continued as Robert's rules of order dictated, and the attendants nominated, seconded, and voted to approve our committee. The meeting adjourned, and Maggie, Amy, and I gathered around Clay.

"First, thank you for agreeing to review Rose's qualifications. I suggest you go to the high school and speak with the principal and maybe some of her teachers. You'll find she possesses an impeccable character."

The next day, we met at the coffee shop for caffeine to go. As we waited for our orders, Amy became quiet. When questioned, she hesitated a second. "Have either of you seen Rose Terry?"

Maggie and I shook our heads.

"The last time I saw Rose was a few weeks ago when she came into Big Ed's with her father. I'm not trying to be ugly—I'm really not. Rose may have natural Bergeron beauty, but she downplays it considerably with her Terry style of fashion." We encouraged Amy to continue. "The Terrys are dear, but they buy their clothes at the same store as their truck tires. Rose is just shy of six feet tall, skinny as a rail, and wears black, thick-framed glasses."

We stared back, mouths open. Did we have time for a beauty queen makeover? Did Rose even want one? I voted to go to the high school as Clay suggested and speak with the principal. Then we could talk to Rose and make some decisions. A sick feeling snaked its way into my stomach, and I dumped my half-full cup of coffee into the trash.

We met with the principal, a wonderful man who gave us the rundown of Miss Rose Terry. She sounded delightful, but I was concerned about Amy's comments. "Sir, do you think Rose is a strong contestant for the festival queen competition?

That man never missed a beat. He looked me squarely in the eye. "If I was on the panel of judges, I'd vote for Rose, hands down." Oh, my stars! If only he had some pull with the judges!

I phoned Rose's mother to schedule our visit. She admitted they'd attended the emergency meeting but snuck out during Clay's rousing speech. She was hesitant but agreed to meet with us. As I hung up, I was puzzled by Rose's reaction. Personally, I found it exciting to be part of an official village project. Who would have guessed Rose and her family didn't feel the same?

Our committee met together outside Rose's home, then strolled to the door. We rang the bell and Rose answered. What exactly had we gotten ourselves into?

The seventeen-year-old standing before us was sporting a black T-shirt tucked into Wrangler jeans. Her blue and black plaid long-sleeved shirt hung limply around her shoulders. Was it my imagination, or had she pulled it out of the dirty clothes and thrown it on? Rose completed her outfit with white athletic socks and no shoes. Our backup beauty queen had pulled her dark-brown hair into a ponytail, probably that morning. Why did I think that? Because it was spilling out of the hairband onto her shoulders.

Amy was right! Square black oversized eyeglasses perched upon her nose, reminding me of the legendary singer/songwriter Buddy Holly. This girl might possess natural beauty, but she did her best to keep it under wraps.

Our hostess ushered us into the living room, and her parents greeted us with proper Southern hospitality. We settled into various couches and chairs while Rose's mother brought in coffee and Louisiana crunch cake. My mother-in-law, Ava, considered her own crunch cake the best in the parish. Would eating this cake be proper Southern etiquette or family betrayal? Maybe I should have a piece, so I could report my findings to Ava? I had two pieces to confirm Ava's was better. Please don't tell her, though.

Rose agreed to represent Graisseville in the festival if we could address a few concerns. First out of the gate was her choice of eyeglasses. Dr. Mercer, in nearby Zachary, could fix up Rose with some contacts. Her mother agreed to call for an appointment the next day, so we moved on to the next issue. Rose voiced the elephant in the room, her lack of fashion sense.

Hmmm...please don't look at me for advice. My idea of fashion was matching my socks to my t-shirt.

Amy piped up. "Oh, sweetie, don't you fret! Aurelie Hebert offered to give you a personal fashion consultation! You girls aren't the same height, not even close, so you can't wear her pageant clothes. But she and her mother offered to take you to Baton Rouge to fix you up with the most fashionable clothing you can afford." Even Amy lost her smile as her words sank in.

The Terrys did not value spending money on clothes, not when the tractor needed new tires. So how would we pay for Rose's pageant clothes?

Maggie came to the rescue. "Hey, ladies, I've got this! My coffee shop's not making a huge profit, but I was just talking to my husband last night, and we agreed to sponsor Rose for the festival. We can use the sponsorship money for clothes." Maggie flashed a grin at Rose. "Consider yourself clothed in pure fashion for the festival!"

Oh my goodness, God solved another problem! Last on our list: the talent competition. Uncle Clay Terry himself said this girl had loads of talent, so we were home free.

Rose's father, like most men, blurted out the obvious. "Yeah, that's fine. But Rose has no talent. What are you going to do about that?"

Thank you, Rose's father, for your positive thinking!

Fortunately, Rose had embraced the Queen of the Festival concept, so she had several ideas. "I have reviewed the rules, and there's a lot of flexibility. My talent can be dancing, vocal, playing an instrument, reciting a monologue, acting, demonstrating, or something else. I think we should focus on the *something else*."

Oh girl, do we want to know what the *something else* could be?

But we needed to. "I can shear a sheep. I can milk a cow. I can whistle *You Are My Sunshine*. I can recite the poem *In the Creole Twilight*. I can call off the capitals of the United States..." She gauged our open mouths and saucer eyes.

Amy again was the voice of reason. "Rose sweetie, didn't your grandma tell me you enjoyed cooking?"

Rose's eyes lit up with excitement. "Yes, but I didn't think that was a festival-worthy talent. Are you saying it is?"

Amy pulled up the rules on her phone, and we gathered around, literally holding our breath. Cooking technically fell under the category of demonstration, so the committee voted to present Rose Terry and our plan to the village in two days. Rose had a fighting chance at the festival as long as she got contacts, took Aurelie Hebert's fashion advice, and cooked a fabulous dish for the judges. It seemed so simple until I lay awake that night in bed. What had I been thinking when I volunteered for the committee? Winning this festival hung on so many variables that we needed a miracle to pull it together.

CHAPTER 16—THE QUEEN OF THE FESTIVAL

We witnessed some amazing transformations as our new Miss Graisseville prepared for her festival challenges. That sweet young lady traded her sturdy glasses for contacts and took advantage of a free cut and bronze highlights from the downtown Bristle 'n' Blush. She accompanied Aurelie Hebert to Baton Rouge for a complimentary fashion consult and a pageant wardrobe courtesy of Maggie's Coffee Shop. The committee was eager to sample Rose's talent, which was her grandmother's shrimp and grits dish.

The dish is a classic recipe enjoyed all over the country, but especially south of the Mason-Dixon line. Grits are a staple among most Southerners, as a substitute for potatoes and rice. Any respectable Southerner eats shrimp and grits regularly, and the Terrys were no exception.

Our community credited Rose's grandmother for creating, hands down, the most delectable shrimp and grits. She guarded her recipe like a state secret, and not even her children had access. Grandmother Terry locked all doors and shut all curtains, leaving no gaps for prying eyes. No one had any clue what took place as she whipped up her shrimp and grits. Our next miracle would be to convince Grandmother Terry to share her recipe. Clay sat down with his mother and lectured her about community spirit. Grandmother Terry didn't budge. Clay brought in his brother (Rose's father) and his sister for reinforcements. The three Terry children called upon family unity, and family history. They ended by describing in great detail how the family could lose this precious recipe forever if Grandmother Terry passed before sharing her secret. The woman shook her head, arms crossed tightly over her chest.

Rose took matters into her own hands. She picked up her grandmother and drove to the cemetery to visit Grandfather Terry's grave. While gazing at her grandfather's tombstone, Rose reminisced about the time she had spent with him. She described their long walks together and how Rose sat in her grandfather's lap while he told her stories of his childhood. Grandmother Terry nodded and wiped a tear from her eye. Rose repeated stories about fishing with her grandfather, always returning with a boatload of catfish.

"You know, Grandma, I wish Grandpa Terry had given me the secret recipe for his catfish bait. Dad and I go to the same place that Grandpa did, but without his secret bait, we don't bring home nearly the number of catfish he did." She looked sideways. Was this woman understanding the conversation?

Grandmother Terry sighed. "Rose, I will give you my shrimp and grits recipe. I don't want my secret to die with me like your grandfather's secret died with him. Oh, glory, that man never let anybody get near the garage when he was cooking up his secret bait! Not even his own wife!" She laughed and gave Rose a hug. "I guess I'm being selfish, but I feel like the recipe is the only thing I have that's still useful. My daughter and daughters-in-law have taken over all the cooking for every family event, except the shrimp and grits. I want to feel needed, and that recipe has been the only way I've been able to do that."

It was Rose's turn to give her grandmother a hug. "Grandma, I cross my heart! I will not share your secret with anyone, and you can still make the shrimp and grits. I feel pretty certain that you will always make them better than me."

Grandmother Terry laughed. "But I have a few conditions." That Grandmother Terry was a shrewd Southern woman. First, she made Rose swear on the family Bible in front of the entire Terry clan that she would never divulge the recipe as long as Grandmother Terry was still breathing. Rose also promised she would never make the shrimp and grits after the festival until Grandmother Terry had passed. Last, Rose promised she would be the only student in Grandmother Terry's cooking lessons, she would not share any information from those lessons, and she would not make any audio or visual recordings during that time. After making these solemn promises, Grandmother Terry granted Rose access to her kitchen.

Grandmother and granddaughter spent most of the six weeks before the festival in the kitchen. Rose first had to memorize not only the recipe but also a new standard of measurement. Grandmother Terry did not use measuring cups or spoons, so Rose had to master "pinch," "smidgen," "dollop," and "dash." She also had to perfect the art of tasting. After she added each ingredient, she tasted the mixture to determine whether the proportions were correct. Rose never had so much fun in her life.

Clay contacted the festival, explained the situation, and listed Rose as our Miss Grais-seville. The committee met with Rose a few days before to give her the once-over and sample her shrimp and grits. Her transformation mesmerized even the most cynical resident. I wasn't sure what Aurelie Hebert planned to do beyond high school, but she had a future as a fairy godmother. That girl seriously worked miracles, and I had already told myself to be on the lookout for some. Miracle number one had been Rose convincing her grandmother to give up her coveted shrimp and grits recipe. Miracle number two was standing before me. Rose had beautiful hazel eyes, hair the color of cinnamon, and a contagious smile. This girl had natural beauty! My sigh rested somewhere between relief and admiration. Our Cinderella was to die for!

She also made shrimp and grits that were heaven on earth. We were there to give final approval on the contestant and the dish, and we left the Terry household believing we had been in the presence of a true beauty. I told Mike later that night I wanted to be buried in Rose's shrimp and grits. His mouth said *okay*, but his eyes said, *I think you're just south of crazy.* He hadn't tasted Rose's shrimp and grits, so he couldn't understand. The entire village attended the festival, including my husband and kids. Mike even closed his store, reasoning that his best customers would be at the festival. The night before, we discussed Rose's excellent chances of winning.

"Honey, what's the name of this festival?"

Mike stared at me. "You mean you don't know?"

Irritated, I snapped. "If I knew, why would I be asking?"

Mike stood in front of me, to have a full view of my reaction as he responded. "Why, it's the Feathers and Fur Festival. That means if Rose wins, her title would be Queen of Feathers and Fur."

We couldn't stop laughing even as we climbed into bed. Still chuckling, I realized God had moved metaphorical mountains so my dark horse could be the Queen of Feathers and Fur.

If only I had stories to tell of the competition and the drama and suspense we endured. Of course, I'd love to say our Rose swept the title hands down. Sadly, she didn't.

Rose was a fierce competitor, but in the end, she was no match for Miss Evangeline Bordelon from Plaquemine (PLACK-UH-MIN) Parish. Evangeline played the harmonica and the piano while singing "Dancing Queen" by ABBA. She also danced while singing and playing the harmonica, thanks to a piano on wheels and harmonica strapped to her chest. What a show-off!

The judges engorged themselves on Rose's shrimp and grits and marveled at her magic hands hiding the ingredients. Yet they still crowned Evangeline Queen of Feathers and Fur. Those obviously biased judges granted Rose First Runner-Up, so I claimed a victory on behalf of my committee. The village hosted a small yet rousing parade for Miss Rose Terry. Mayor Ruby dug up some funds and posted a tasteful billboard just outside the village limits. It read "Village of Graisseville: Home of First Runner-Up Queen of Feathers and Fur." A definite step toward economic growth.

CHAPTER 17 – THE MOST INTERESTING PARADE

Louisiana is full of history and culture, with Mardi Gras definitely a part of that. The words "Mardi Gras" are French for "Fat Tuesday," reflecting the practice of gorging on decadent food the last night before Lent. There is so much history regarding Mardi Gras that I won't try to relate even a small part. I will just say that when you live in Louisiana, celebrate Mardi Gras with food, parties, and most definitely a parade.

Mike and I had never celebrated Mardi Gras together, and I was excited about the upcoming parade. Maggie burst my bubble.

"Oh, that's normally hosted by the merchants' association. But they aren't doing it this year."

What? No Mardi Gras parade? That hurt my heart, and I vowed to bring it up at the next council meeting.

I'd always been fascinated with politics, so I attended the monthly village council meetings. Was my attendance appreciated? Probably not, but I was never turned away. It was a public forum, and I considered myself part of the public. During the section called public comment, I took my stand.

"Mayor, members of the council, I am deeply saddened at the absence of our Mardi Gras parade. As a member of this community, I am offering my leadership skills. In my short time in Graisseville, I organized a nativity scene that shattered all previous attendance records. I have championed the election of the First Runner Up Queen of

Feathers and Fur. Some would call me a rainmaker of sorts, a mover and a shaker in the community."

Ignoring the eye rolls, I continued. "As a resident, I am deeply concerned that the council has dismissed the annual Mardi Gras Parade. Just because the merchants aren't interested, doesn't mean we should toss the entire event! As a leader in this community, I have a large amount of interest in this parade's success." I was woman, hear me roar! Hmmm...did I hear chuckling in the background?

"Mayor, deputy sheriff, Board of Aldermen, and distinguished guests! I would like to volunteer as chairperson for the Mardi Gras Parade. This event is part of Graisseville's history, and I want to continue this fine tradition." My eyes scanned the room for support. Why were there so many uninterested faces?

My ally, Clay Terry, took up my charge. "Thank you, Miss Jen! I make a motion to approve Mrs. Jen Guidry as chairperson of our annual Mardi Gras Parade. All in favor, say, aye!"

Just like that, I was in charge of our Mardi Gras Parade. Maggie had to share my good news! On my way home I dialed her number.

"Oh, Jen, you didn't! Please tell me you didn't!"

"What? This is great news! Why are you upset?"

"Under any other mayor, I'd say go for it! But in the regime of Mayor Ruby, a parade is next to impossible. The merchants refuse to participate because of Ruby's ridiculous restrictions. We can't throw candy or gum from the floats—too much sugar. The only acceptable food items are healthy ones or nonedible items. You know, beads, doubloons, plastic cups."

How could we have a parade without candy?

"Ruby's also banned Mardi Gras staples like King Cake, beignets, pancakes, Po' boy sandwiches, and dirty rice."

Why hadn't I talked to Maggie before volunteering?

"Oh, she went even further. Ruby banned motorized floats in the parade. She claims the engine fumes are detrimental to the environment, because of all the stopping and starting. Every entry in the parade has to travel by foot, bicycle, or animal. Oh, electric bicycles and cars are acceptable. But who owns one of those?"

No wonder the merchants backed out. But I was still woman, and I still roared.

"We can make this work! I'll be at the coffee shop's doorstep bright and early tomorrow morning. Surely these two amazingly smart youngish women can figure this out!"

After dropping off the boys, my laptop and I parked at a corner table to scour the internet. My mission: find eco- and family-friendly parades. As Maggie and her crew served the morning rush, my internet results fell together. By the time 9:00 a. m. rolled around, the shop had emptied and I was ready for my presentation.

"Maggie, I think I've got it! We're going to have a Mardi Gras Parade for pets!"

Her eyebrows shot to the top of her forehead, black caterpillars registering uncertainty.

"No, this is going to be great! Any pet owner can enter their pet as long as it's on a leash or in a cage. Humans and pets can wear costumes, and even dress alike."

The caterpillars relaxed a bit. "I'll have final approval of all the pets, so we won't have any dangerous ones."

The caterpillars nestled back down, and I could see lights in Maggie's eyes. "Jen, this could be a lot of fun! My girls will enter our dog, and I can dress them up in matching costumes. Oh, I think this will be fabulous!"

Maggie threw in a few ideas of her own. "What about throwing pet treats to the crowd? And small pet toys too!"

We knocked out advertising, created an entry form, and typed up the rules. As I left to work at my real job, I knew this parade would be a hit. But what about final approval?

"Clay? This is Jen Guidry. Sorry to bother you at work, but could we discuss the details of the parade?"

Clay embraced my pet parade concept. "Jen, this is just a fabulous idea! My grandkids have pets ranging from hamsters to birds to dogs. They are going to love this!" Mission accomplished!

After supper, I cleared the kitchen while Mike supervised bath time.

My cell phone rang with an unknown number.

"Miss Jen? This here is Shorty Cormier. I heard about yore pet parade, and I was wantin' tuh know if a pig can be in it. See, my nephew Bubba has a pet pig, and he'd sure like tuh be in the parade. Bubba that is. I'm not sure how the pig feels."

A pig can't be that bad, especially if it's a pet. "Of course! You can pick up an entry form at Maggie's coffee shop."

"Yes, ma'am—we'll surely do that. Thank ya for yer time."

My first entry without even advertising! Small towns have their own form of advertising, something that money can't buy.

Mardi Gras is officially the Tuesday before Ash Wednesday, making Mardi Gras forty-seven days before Easter. We'd scheduled the parade the Saturday before Fat Tuesday, which made it at the tail end of February. The weather in Louisiana was normally balmy that time of the year, so I had high hopes for a sunny and warm parade.

Two weeks before go time I had thirty-seven entries. Most were dogs and cats, but I had my fair share of hamsters, guinea pigs, and lizards. Not to mention the Cormier's pig, a miniature donkey, a pygmy goat, some hedgehogs, and a deodorized skunk. Originally, I'd vetoed spiders and snakes, but the owners threatened to go to the Board of Aldermen claiming discrimination. We couldn't have people protesting the parade or filing any type of lawsuit, so I welcomed them with open arms.

Since our downtown was tiny, most parades went around the block twice. This surprisingly large parade wouldn't need that second time.

Several horse owners contacted me, and I realized I needed some sort of animal cleanup crew. Who could I convince to take on that task? Deputy Chris Landry saved the day.

"Don't worry, Miss Jen. Why I'll get the sheriff to authorize Parade Poop Duty as community service. There'll be at least three or four people needing service hours that weekend."

Roby Melancon called to enter his alligator. In the interest of inclusion, I said yes, as long as it was contained. Remember the guy who owned the camel? He called to enter her in the parade. My veto power had flown out the window. I said yes to everyone, and word got around. We had a raccoon, a bat, a wolf-dog hybrid, a hawk, and an assortment of parakeets, canaries, and parrots. My parade had seventy-two entries, so I cut off registration at seventy-five. As long as the owners contained their animals, what could go wrong?

Another strange number popped on my screen. "Mrs. Guidry, my name is Millie Taylor, and I own a bakery here in Baton Rouge. I'm branching out to animal treats and calling it Little Nibbles. Could I rent an outdoor space at the parade and sell my pet goodies? I can bake animal-safe treats that taste like king cake, beignets, cinnamon rolls, and pecan pralines—all for pets."

"Why, of course! You'd be a delightful addition to the parade."

My excitement knew no bounds! I'd observed all of Ruby's rules, and we still were going to have a wonderful parade.

Mike gave me some walkie-talkies from Big Ed's and volunteered to work crowd control while Ava and Walt watched the kids. Deputy Chris called for a couple of reinforcements, but they just stood around shooting the breeze with my husband.

Maggie and I spent one night researching which animals were predators of which animals in the parade. Thank goodness for the internet! We sorted out our parade lineup, making sure all animals who liked to eat other animals were as far away as possible from the animals they enjoyed eating.

My pet owners did not disappoint. The parade finished with no casualties or altercations, animal or otherwise. Our participants included a camel and a sheik, dogs and cats dressed like their human counterparts, and a skunk in a stroller wearing a baby gown and bonnet. The alligator was contained in a tank with a mannequin arm sticking out of the murky water and a sign that read, "Do Not Feed the Alligator." We never saw the bat since it was daylight, but his owners created a bat house straight out of the Garden District in New Orleans. That bat was the envy of his friends!

The cute little pink pig turned out to be a 150-pound hog sporting a top hat and monocle. Everyone declared the parade a great success.

The baker from Baton Rouge was related to Clay Terry on his mother's side. Clay had contacted his cousin about the business opportunity, and she turned a tidy profit that day.

She put in a request for a booth at the next pet parade. "The trek was definitely worth it! We sold out of king cake and beignets, and I have just a few cinnamon rolls and pecan pralines to load. Thanks again!"

I caught Maggie's eye as she supervised the Pooper Scooper Patrol.

"Hey, girl, we did it! We pulled off the most fabulous Mardi Gras Parade in the history of Graisseville! I am so proud of us!" As I put my arm around her, I noticed a beignet sticking out of a Little Nibbles bag. My friend shoved it into her purse but said nothing.

"Maggie, why are you eating animal treats? Are you that hungry?" Maggie dug through her purse, ignoring my questions.

My husband walked up holding a Little Nibbles bag, yet we didn't own any pets.

"Okay, guys, what is going on?"

My friend and my husband looked at me, then at each other, then back at me. Who would break first?

"Well, here's the thing, Jen, my dear—my best friend. Clay Terry's cousin wasn't really selling pet treats. She was selling people treats. Clay explained she'd have to disguise her baked goods as animal food. To be fair, no one in town realized what was going on until they walked up to the booth. Clay coached her on who to trust with her secret." My friend stopped, both she and my husband searching for my approval.

Hmmm...did I ever see any pets eating Little Nibbles? "Okay, that was pure genius! I'll tip my imaginary hat in Clay Terry's direction. That man knows how to work the system."

By the grace of God, I'd pulled off my third relatively complex activity in the community.

Mike and I piled into my Jeep with the boys and headed to the Dairy Delight. As we devoured our frozen treats, Henry expressed his approval of the parade.

"Mom, that was hands down the best parade I've ever seen. It was even better than the Christmas parade in Dallas."

My skin felt warm from basking in my kindergartener's praise.

"But, Mom, I was thinking. James and I should be in the parade next year, and we need a pet for that. Grandma said she'd buy whatever animal we wanted. I've talked it over with James, and we want an alligator. When can we pick it up?" Mike conveniently focused all his attention on his root beer float.

"Well, Henry, I'm sure you and your father and grandmother can figure that out tomorrow. For now, let's just enjoy our ice cream." My son worked on his cone, satisfied with my answer.

Best to give Mike my opinion on the kids' pet choices. "You know it's either me or the alligator, right?"

Mike paused, spoon in midair. His brown eyes met mine. "Honey, I'll take you over an alligator any day."

CHAPTER 18—RUBY SPRUCES UP THE TOWN

M ike convinced the boys to adopt a pet needing a good home, like one from the animal shelter. An alligator already had a good home, and probably family and friends that he would miss. Fortunately for us, five- and three-year-old boys make decisions easy to influence. We just needed to find time to go to the animal shelter.

I was in the coffee shop one morning when our mayor burst through the doors. I had never seen her so excited, or even a little excited, for that matter.

"Ladies, I just had to share our good fortune! A national television show called *Small Town Tales* is coming to Graisseville!" Ruby's were dancing, maybe even a little crazed.

I had never heard of the show and most people still considered me pretty ignorant, so I broke the awkward silence. "I'm sorry, Ruby, I've never watched *Small Town Tales*. What's it about?"

The mayor shot me an exasperated look, then launched into a three-minute explanation.

"Well, you see, Jen, It's a national show! A fine young man named Jacob Kettleman is the host, and he visits a small town each week. Now, this industrious member of society started in his small hometown in Mississippi. But he's branched out across the South. And he's chosen us for his next show! He's coming to Graisseville in two weeks! He's going to interview me of course, and other elected officials. He might interview some of our more important residents and downtown business owners." Ruby's feet moved back and forth as if she had an imaginary dance partner. More important residents? Would that be me?

"Anyway, I've called an emergency village council meeting for tonight. With only two weeks to prepare, we've got to get moving!"

Wild horses wouldn't stop me from that meeting, and Mike was happy to stay home with the boys. "Of course, honey. I'll feed them pepperoni pizza from the Gas 'n' More, and we'll play video games until bath time. We love guys' night in."

My bestie wanted in on the fun, so I picked her up from the coffee shop on the way. She had two cups of coffee for us, and that was why she was my best friend.

Ruby painted a picture of the opportunities a nationally syndicated show could bring our village. "And on this chart, you can see the increase in economic growth once our episode hits the airwaves. And on this graph, you can see it in green—for money."

Weren't the numbers pointless? The woman had no data. There were no studies on the growth of revenue in a small town after being featured on television. I had to hand it to her though because everyone else drooled over her PowerPoint presentation. Once they saw her charts and graphs, they voted to reallocate village funds. They also authorized Ruby to make improvements and repairs to the village as she deemed appropriate—with no oversight. Business owners, including Maggie, shot up from their seats to donate money. What was that smell? Oh yes, the smell of imminent disaster.

After saying prayers and kissing the boys good night, I filled Mike in on Ruby's ridiculous meeting. "Honey, she created the charts and graphs from imaginary information! They were the most unrealistic projections—a four hundred percent increase in revenue for all businesses. Why couldn't anyone else see that?"

"No idea honey. But I don't think she was trying to deceive anyone. Do you?"

"No, she wants what's best for our village. But she has her eye on the prize, which is looking good on television. In her mind, the end justifies the means." How would the village improvement project play out?

Ruby formed a committee. "People, we've got to make sure our projects will be completed by our two-week deadline." There were six of us, but we didn't do anything. Ruby chose the improvements and repairs, ordered the supplies, and hired the contractors to complete the work. "In the interest of time, I'll take care of everything. We can meet back in a couple of weeks and I'll update you."

Some improvements made nice changes to our community. Additional landscaping in the park, new playground equipment, a freshly painted gazebo, more park benches, murals on the park bathrooms, and sky-blue trash cans were all welcome improvements.

Some of Ruby's projects would have been ideal in a larger community. But in a town of 298 residents, they made no sense. Our mayor took a portion of our village park and fenced it off for dogs.

Each business offered free maps that folded up and fit in a convenient carrying case. "Mike, who's going to use them? Most visitors just pass through, or they're here to visit family. And the top of the map is east! Tourists would be better off using their GPS or asking for directions."

Mike kept one eye on the television. "Jen, you're right—you don't need me to tell you that. But what can we do? Let's just ride this out and see what happens."

Our village installed a bicycle lane that ran the entire two blocks of downtown, work-out equipment and circuit stations in the park, and bookshelves with free books on all four corners of downtown. Most were nice amenities to have, and many were frivolous. But they could not hold a candle to the rest of the projects our fine mayor authorized.

Ruby hired her nephew as the village troubadour, performing hourly five nights a week. Thanks to an amazing deal at a lighting store, all the trees in the park and downtown displayed chandeliers of various sizes and shapes. Ruby had enough chandeliers left over to decorate most of the trees in the historic district. There were no electrical outlets, so the lights hung forlornly in the trees. Because of a fantastic sale on outdoor seating, every corner displayed some sort of bench or table and chairs.

Ruby hired Shorty Cormier and Roby Melancon as public transportation drivers and tour guides. The village map displayed the stops, and on the back was the schedule. Village funds paid for Shorty and Roby to paint their trucks orange, which coordinated with navy uniforms embroidered with *Graisseville Public Transportation and Tours*. The men drove their trucks on a scheduled route five days a week, and on weekends they were available as tour guides.

If a visitor didn't appreciate the rigidity of public transportation, there were thirty free sky-blue bicycles parked neatly in matching sky-blue racks downtown.

"Mike, I am beyond frustrated! Ruby is spending ridiculous amounts of money."

"Yes, you're right, honey. But what can we do?"

The boys tumbled into the house, out of breath from playing in the front yard. "Mom! Dad! There's a puppy in our yard! Can we keep her?"

Mike and I ran outside, greeted by a young dog looking like a mix of boxer and Labrador retriever. Mike inspected the dog while trying not to get licked.

"The boys are right, she's a girl, and I don't see a collar. We should take her to the vet. You know, have her checked out and see if she's chipped. We should also put up some signs and see if anyone's missing her. I'll put one up at the store. Why don't you take one to Maggie?"

"All right. But boys, don't get attached—she probably belongs to someone." Yeah, Jen. While you're at it, tell them to stop breathing. Both instructions would be impossible.

Henry piped up. "What's my teacher's name, Mom?"

What a strange question. "Mrs. Mathers."

An eye roll—something new that was becoming a habit. "No, Mom, what's her first name?"

"Sadie, I think. And don't roll your eyes at me."

"Sorry. I'm going to call our dog Sadie too."

Oh my stars, this was the beginning of the end. We were going to keep the dog, or my kids would nurse broken hearts.

"Henry, why would you name a dog after your teacher?"

Another eye roll, but he changed it into blinking. "Because if someone names their dog after you, well, that's the greatest honor you could ever get."

Interesting logic, but sweet. I'd ignore the eye roll.

Henry didn't name the dog Sadie too as in Sadie as well. He named the dog Sadie Two, the second Sadie in Henry's life.

"Honey, don't let me forget to call the vet and make an appointment for Sadie Two. Let's make up a few signs."

We passed out the signs but forgot the vet.

The production crew for *Small Town Tales* was scheduled to arrive, and a large crowd formed just inside the village limits. I was there, of course, with Mike and Maggie. All eight of the local businesses were represented, The mayor, all three aldermen, and Deputy Landry stood in the front. The parish sheriff was there too along with three other deputies for crowd control. That was one smart sheriff—all five officers had their hands full. School had been let out for the day, so most of the faculty and students were in attendance. The band director of the Graisseville High School Fighting Mules marching band had brought his complete entourage—seven band members, three cheerleaders, two majorettes, and the new mascot, Leroy II. All we were missing was a partridge in a pear tree.

No doubt we scared the production crew, who drove up in a burgundy minivan. Jacob Kettleman was an extremely energetic young man, and by our estimations, not much older than twenty-five. His brother and his iPhone were the production crew.

We welcomed Jacob and Chase with the "Star-Spangled Banner" and the Louisiana state song, "You Are My Sunshine". The Fighting Mules' fight song was to the tune of *"You Are My Sunshine"*. No one had put much thought into that part of the program.

"Welcome Jacob Kettleman and the production crew of *Small Town Tales*! By the authority invested in me by the village of Graisseville, Louisiana, I pronounce this day *Small Town Tales Day.*"

Ruby presented both young men with T-shirts featuring our village map on the back, with east at the top. Mike leaned over. "Let's hope they don't try to use their shirts to find their way around town!" The front of the shirts had a picture of Leroy II. Or was it Leroy the Original? Did it even matter?

"Now let's get this show on the road! Follow me, boys!" The mayor climbed into a Graisseville Public Transportation and Tours vehicle, also known as Roby's orange truck. The convoy drove toward downtown. "Now, I must insist you leave your minivan here—I promise it will be safe! Hop into our Graisseville Public Transportation and Tours vehicle. You're in for a treat! We'll start with a detailed tour of the village."

Mike headed to the store for a late opening, but this girl had to stick around and watch the fun. I waited patiently, skipping the tour of the village. According to the itinerary, next up was the interview with the mayor. Then the three aldermen, and two of the eight business owners. Maggie's Coffee Shop made the list along with the *Gazette*. Mike was relieved he didn't make the cut.

Ruby had a six-foot table set up in the park with a white canopy to protect everyone from the elements. What the heck? A Shetland pony, a donkey, three goats, two sheep, chickens, ducks, and bunny rabbits wandered around the dog park while a camel stepped off a truck. Curious, I walked over and spotted a sign proclaiming *Graisseville Complimentary Petting Zoo*. Seriously, Ruby? That woman had rented a petting zoo! How much did that cost? No, Jen—you didn't want to know.

My next stop was the coffee shop—knowing Ruby, the tour of Graisseville would take at least an hour. Maggie whipped up one of her March specialty drinks, a Lucky Leprechaun featuring pistachio flavoring. As my friend blended the drink, she gushed. The girl had nothing on Annelise and the fountain in Audubon Park.

"Oh, Jen, isn't this so exciting? I can't believe we're going to be on TV! I'm going to be on TV! Does my hair look okay?"

Much as I tried to be excited, the whole experience screamed *ridiculousness*. If *Small Town Tales* didn't like our community, who cared?

Oh, Jen—you've become one of them. You've become one of the collective, a small town resident proud of your community and all that it offered. No, I didn't care what anyone thought about my village because I liked it just the way it was. Well, the way it used to be before Ruby made all her ridiculous improvements.

After two hours, Roby's truck pulled into the park. Sipping my green caffeinated creation, I strolled over to watch the interview. Should I ride one of the thirty sky-blue bikes sitting outside the coffee shop? Since the park was just fifty yards away, I chose to walk.

Reclining on one of the forty-two benches a few feet from the interview table, I scanned the park. As the crew fastened a microphone on Ruby, I pondered. Had there also been a fabulous sale on outdoor park benches? With no less than forty-two, it seemed a sure bet. And what would the park look like if all forty-two benches were occupied? Ruby's interview began, but my thoughts continued to wander. What would happen if the animals broke out of the petting zoo? Would Jacob and Chase pull out their iPhones and start filming? Would Deputy Landry pursue on foot or in his banana-colored smart car? Would Maggie's traffic increase as people flocked downtown to watch the chaos? If I pulled out my phone and filmed, would my video go viral?

Before I'd finished my daydream, Ruby's interview was over, and the three aldermen were taking the stage. What was that strange vibe coming from Jacob and Chase? As much as I tried, I couldn't put my finger on it.

CHAPTER 19—RUBY EATS CROW

Even though I'd daydreamed, I trained one eye on the interview. I never saw any phones or cameras, just Jacob plugging her microphone into a digital recorder. Ruby sat beside me, the only audience for the show.

"Ruby, I never saw a camera during your interview. Don't you think that's strange?"

"Jen, you're being too technical. These fine young entrepreneurs took plenty of videos during their tour of Graisseville. They are professionals, who've produced countless shows. Have any of us ever produced any national television shows? Now shush...I want to hear this!"

My mind focused on things I could control. Our flyers for Sadie Two were unsuccessful. Or successful, depending on whether you were me or Henry and James.

"Did you hear that, Sadie Two? We get to keep you!"

"Yes, but she can't come inside the house until we take her to the vet. And she could still have a chip, which means the vet can contact her owner."

My nightly prayers were pleas for the boys. Lord, please don't let this dog have a chip. I don't want to watch two hearts break.

Mike and I miscommunicated, not unusual among most married couples.

"I thought you were taking her to the vet."

"No, I definitely asked you to take her. We have a big sale on insecticide this month."

I scheduled another appointment and marked it on my calendar. The vet had plenty of time in his schedule, but I had multiple deadlines looming.

Sadie Two's ribs had disappeared, and her coat was healthier and shinier. "Boys, this dog should only be eating her dog food and special treats. No human food." The dog had gained a good six pounds, probably from the boys sneaking snacks for their new best friend. My mind drifted back to my work deadlines, and I forgot about our chubby visitor.

Ruby rented a twenty-foot projection screen, so we could view our fifteen minutes of fame in high definition. She hired Dillon to perform with the Graisseville High School Fighting Mules marching band. Maggie was open before the watch party, and we all crowded into her shop for coffee and pastries. Despite our frustration, Mike and I were excited to watch the latest episode of *Small Town Tales*. We disagreed with Ruby's extravagant use of village funds, but we were looking forward to seeing our hometown and our friends on national television.

Ruby's grandson, Ethan, the one who handled the village's social media, was in charge of getting the episode on the projection screen. Ruby received the link a few days before but refused to send it to her grandson. "It's top secret, Ethan, even from you!"

Ten minutes before the watch party, she handed her phone to her grandson. His job was to sort through his grandmother's emails, find the link, and put it on the projection screen. Ethan had been dealing with Ruby and her lack of technology skills for many years, so we didn't anticipate any problems.

The watch party coincided with sunset, so we could be enveloped in darkness like a movie theater. Ruby rented a popcorn machine and hired people to hand out bags. We sat and munched on our salted buttery goodness, wondering why the screen was still dark. Fifteen minutes after *Small Town Tales* was to begin, Ruby came over a loudspeaker.

"Ladies and gentlemen, I thank you for your patience. It has come to my attention that *Small Town Tales* is actually a podcast, not a television show. For those of you who, like myself, are unfamiliar with a podcast, my grandson Ethan will explain."

Next came Ethan's voice, with a definite tone of exasperation. "So a podcast is a digital audio file that you can download to any device. A podcast doesn't have any video. It's just people talking."

Ah, that weird vibe I got from Jacob and Chase! Those young men spent their entire visit wondering why we were so wound up about a podcast. They didn't know these small-town residents thought we were part of a television show. No wonder they seemed confused at the outrageousness. As the realization set in, Mike and I had to laugh. What else could we do? It didn't last long, because we were the only ones laughing.

Ethan played the podcast and found a nice picture of our downtown to put on the screen. The photo was before Ruby's improvements, but it was still a nice photo to gaze upon as we listened. It was a wonderful podcast, all things considered. Ruby sounded mayoral, and the aldermen sounded...well, however, aldermen should sound. Maggie was her fabulous self during her interview, and Hugh Cormier represented the newspaper and the village in a charming and knowledgeable manner. Our fellow residents did not share our appreciation and demanded, of all things, an emergency town council meeting. Mike and I felt sorry for Ruby.

On the home front, I rescheduled the vet appointment. My boss had piled another deadline on my plate, and I wanted my evening free for the emergency meeting. As I wrote the appointment on the calendar, I added a note to ask about nutrition. Sadie Two was becoming pleasantly plump.

Walt offered to watch the boys, so Mike and I could attend the meeting. We left in plenty of time. The meeting was going to be crowded.

Poor Ruby! Her normally perfect makeup was streaked with tears. Her husband Al sat beside her holding her hand. Al Bergeron was a man short in stature yet tall in patience. From the look on his face, his patience had shrunk a few inches. The three aldermen and Deputy Landry were there, with faces better suited for a hanging. Ruby's hanging maybe?

Clay called the meeting to order and led the assault. He threw the proverbial book at Ruby and demanded her resignation. The other two aldermen threw in their two cents' worth and made a motion to accept Ruby's resignation, although Ruby hadn't offered it. Deputy Landry remained silent. Although Mike disagreed, I wanted to defend Ruby. I raised my hand, and Clay called on me. He probably thought I would side with the majority, so he felt safe in letting me speak.

"Thank you, Alderman. I'd like to add a few words. I agree—Ruby went completely overboard. But she was not the only guilty party. The aldermen recommended the real-location of funds, without confirming Ruby's data. They authorized the improvements with no oversight. Why they even encouraged business owners to donate funds." Judging from the faces, I wasn't winning any admirers.

"And the rest of us—we should also be held accountable." Mike scanned the room, looking for the nearest exit. His eyes screamed *why didn't you keep your mouth shut*?

"We, the residents of Graisseville, are responsible, to some degree. None of us bothered to check up on *Small Town Tales*. If just one of us had typed the name into a search browser, we would have discovered it's a successful national podcast. Not a television show."

I don't remember the rest of the speech, but it included the Thomas Jefferson quote, "Every government degenerates when trusted to the rulers of the people alone. The people themselves are its only safe depositories." If President Jefferson was alive, he would have told me to keep my mouth shut.

As I returned to my seat, I didn't hear any applause. I wasn't surprised to see my husband and mother-in-law on their feet, headed for the door. As I searched the silent room, I saw some faces less angry and more thoughtful. After an awkward pause of at least fifteen seconds, Ruby stood up and smiled at me.

"My fellow Americans, I realize you put a great deal of trust in me when you over-whelmingly elected me your mayor. I broke your trust when I didn't research Jacob Kettleman and his podcast program. This caused me to inappropriately divert village funds for extravagant improvement projects. After speaking with my husband, I have decided it is in the best interest of the village for me to step down

as your mayor." Ruby took a breath. "I have five months left in my term. According to the village bylaws, if a mayor has six months or less remaining in a term, the appointed mayor pro tem will step in to serve the remaining months. When I took office, I appointed Clay Terry as the mayor pro tem."

Ruby shakily smiled at Clay and motioned him to stand. "Ladies and gentlemen, I'd like to present your new mayor." Ruby began to clap, and the rest of us slowly joined her.

Clay thanked Ruby and the council. He promised to present his plan for rebuilding the village bank account at the next council meeting. Then he adjourned the meeting, and we made our way to our respective cars.

We were silent during the ride to Walt and Ava's. We dropped off Ava and gathered up the boys, but we didn't stay long. I had so many thoughts going through my head that I couldn't organize them into a single cohesive thought.

On the way home, Mike and I processed our thoughts. For all Ruby's faults, we thought she got railroaded. We were concerned about our village and whether it could survive without a cushion of funds in the bank. We liked Clay very much and hoped he could lead us in a new direction of prosperity. Mike suggested we pray on the way home.

"Lord, please guide our new mayor and show him the best path to lead us out of this mess. Please be with Ruby and her family. Bring them peace and comfort as Ruby transitions out of office. Amen."

My heart weighed two pounds less as we pulled into the driveway. The boys wanted to say good night to Sadie Two, so Mike took them outside as I brewed a cup of coffee. I'd earned it!

As I sat on the couch and kicked off my shoes, I reflected upon the last twelve months. Just a year ago on that very couch, my husband told me he couldn't breathe. I played fruit basket turnover with my life, convinced I was sacrificing so much for the man I loved. As I sipped my coffee, I had an epiphany of sorts. When I compared what I lost to what I gained, I found the total overwhelming.

In my lost column was a coffee shop on every corner, a beautiful home, and unlimited shopping opportunities. But in the win column, I had the best specialty coffee shop five minutes from my home. And the bonus of my best friend as the owner.

In my win column was an equally beautiful home with five acres for my boys to just run. Maggie and I had taken multiple girls' trips to Baton Rouge. We'd shopped, laughed, and deepened our friendship. Yes, I'd lost countless restaurants within minutes. But I'd gained dinner every night with my family because my husband had a shorter commute and fewer hours in his workweek.

I no longer attended my church of seven years with good friends and an amazing pastor, but I had gained a new church also filled with good friends and an amazing pastor. I had lost my bright lights but gained a yard filled with lightning bugs. Tears prickled in the corners of my eyes as I thanked God for my overflowing cup.

My men burst into the living room, and I wiped away my tears. Mike understood that women cry for no obvious reason, but the kids didn't get it. I made a mental note to discuss my overflowing cup with Mike and thank him for bringing me to my new hometown.

Henry and James jumped up and down. "Mom! Mom! You'll never guess what's happening! Sadie Two has puppies coming out of her booty!"

My eyes searched Mike's face, but he just shrugged. Yeah, I was going to need a bigger cup.

Also By Jann Franklin

**You can find my books on Amazon or my website.   Happy shop- ping!

Small Town Girl Series

Jen's life isn't perfect, but it's beautiful. A beautiful mess.

Jen was living her best big city life, until her husband Mike uproots them to small town Louisiana. Life throws you curveballs, but you've got to keep swinging. This heartwarming series resonates with joyful, almost nostalgic feelings of encourage-ment. Readers living in big cities will feel the quaint, small-town Southern charm leaping off the pages, and experience a yearning to visit their very own Graisseville. And readers from small towns will see versions of themselves and their own community in these characters, nodding and laughing along with Jen and her family. There is something for everyone to relate to and thoughtfully consider.

Trading Bright Lights for Lightning Bugs

Shining Stars and Mason Jars

Cheese Grits and Hissy Fits

Small Town Girl Mystery Series

Why is murder so much fun?

Evangeline Delafose found Graisseville, Louisiana just as she remembered—boring and uneventful. Until she solved a murder. Now she's hooked.

Follow Ev as she takes on each mystery, with her frustrating but loveable private investigator by her side. And, of course, a bit of insider info from the quirky residents of her small town.

You'll laugh, cry and roll your eyes at the antics of this charming small-town Southern sleuth and her exasperating private investigator.

Muffalettas and Murder

Boudin and Bloodshed

Fruitcake and Fraud

Mardi Gras and Mayhem

Sweet Tea and Suspects

ABOUT JANN

Jann Franklin lives in the small town of Grand Cane, Louisiana. Over three hundred other people also live in Grand Cane, and many of Jann's chapters came from her weekly visits at the downtown coffee shop. She would like it on the record that Grand Cane's current mayor and aldermen are nothing like the characters in her book. They are definitely larger than life, but in a good way.

She and her husband John enjoy Sundays at Grand Cane Baptist Church, dinner with family and friends, and watching the lightning bugs in their backyard. Their kids come to visit, when they aren't too busy living their big-city lives.

She graduated from high school in Russellville, another small town in Arkansas. She obtained her accounting degree from Baylor University in Waco, Texas and moved to Dallas in 1989. She still dabbles in accounting but has taken up writing to satisfy her creative side. Like Jen Guidry, she never appreciated her small-town upbringing until she was encouraged to move back to one. Now she cannot imagine living any other way.

If you ever make it to Grand Cane, stop by By Faith Coffee House and say "hi." They make amazing coffee, and they will save a seat and a smile for you.

Made in the USA
Monee, IL
05 November 2024

69413326R00069